Prai

"Powerful . . . a
—*KIRKUS REVIEWS*

"Raschke interprets motifs of loss, separation, and renewal with keen storytelling chops and a distinctive lyrical style. This brief but riveting story has much to offer."
—*PUBLISHERS WEEKLY*

"A mercilessly taut, relentlessly thrilling tale of heartbreak and survival. Raschke writes with humanity and grace about the challenges of parenthood, and the rigors of the natural world."
—JONATHAN EVISON, author of *Lawn Boy* and
The Revised Fundamentals of Caregiving

"*To the Mountain* pits a father and son against the wilderness survival tale's usual merciless elements: perilous trails, menacing predators, and poor cell reception. What lifts this novel above the ordinary also challenges readers—to enter the hyper-sensory perspective of the autistic boy as he puzzles his way through an insensate world. It is not a spoiler to say that love matters when the odds seem insurmountable and surrender feels like mercy."
—CHARLIE QUIMBY, author of *Monument Road*
and *Inhabited*

"A deeply affecting tale of a father's love for his autistic son. Erik Raschke's lyrical prose evokes both the awesome wilderness of the Rocky Mountains in winter and the unfathomable wilderness of the human heart. This brief and beautiful novel will linger long after you have turned the last page."

—MARGARET COEL, *New York Times* bestselling author of *Winter's Child*

To the Mountain

To the Mountain

a novel

Erik Raschke

TORREY HOUSE PRESS

SALT LAKE CITY • TORREY

This is a work of fiction. Any resemblance to actual events or persons, living or dead, is entirely coincidental.

First Torrey House Press Edition, February 2021
Copyright © 2021 by Erik Raschke

Published by Torrey House Press
Salt Lake City, Utah
www.torreyhouse.org

International Standard Book Number: 978-1-948814-32-4
E-book ISBN: 978-1-948814-33-1
Library of Congress Control Number: 2019955117

Cover art by David Shingler
Cover design by Kathleen Metcalf
Interior design by Rachel Buck-Cockayne
Distributed to the trade by Consortium Book Sales and Distribution

Torrey House Press offices in Salt Lake City sit on the homelands of Ute, Goshute, Shoshone, and Paiute nations. Offices in Torrey are in homelands of Paiute, Ute, and Navajo nations.

For Kes

When you saw, far off, the heavy fate approaching, did you not say to the mountains, "hide me," to the hills, "fall on me"? Or if you were stronger, did your feet nevertheless not drag you along the way? Did they not hanker, as it were, to get back into the old tracks? When you were called, did you answer, or did you not? Perhaps softly and in a whisper? Not so Abraham, gladly, boldly trustingly he answered out loud "here I am."

—Søren Kierkegaard, *Fear and Trembling*

I

Marshall could not remember how time or the calendar worked, so he was never sure what day it was. In the juvenile center, he could tell the time of day by the smells emanating from the kitchen. Leading up to dinner, there was meat roasting, pasta boiling, and vegetables steaming. After dinner, those smells gave way to soap, and cold food mixed in open trash cans.

Now, he was sure it was gym time and this was confirmed when the attendants told him to stop playing with his Duplos and change his clothes. He stood reluctantly and, as he walked down the hall to the gym, he sensed that the weekend was approaching by the way the attendants chatted in an easy manner, leaning their bodies against walls and texting frequently.

***

When Marshall arrived at the indoor gym courts, the other boys were already shouting, slamming balls against the cement floor. Their voices condensed, ricocheting from tiles, benches, and cement walls, swirling into a single din. He plugged his ears with his fingers, but he needed his hands to change into his gym clothes. He went to the locker room, unplugged his ears, took off his shoes, clasped his hands to his head, and pulled down his pants. With all the noise coming from the gym, it was impossible to think through the task: take off shoes, take off pants, pull on shorts. He took off his underwear, put his shoes on backward. The sequence of steps whirred and jumbled in his mind.

Eventually, he stumbled into the gym, and as he joined the scattered melee, someone tapped his shoulder then ran off. Boys were running past, bumping, hurrah-ing. The whistle blew and they condensed into assigned rows. A boy whose broad face and shaved head was disproportionate to the gentleness of his gait whispered a threat into Marshall's ear, each consonant like a breeze through lake reeds.

***

It was nearing the end of winter in Colorado, when storms transitioned from sullen to boisterous to soggy. The spring clouds occasionally coalesced, loosed damp, unstoppable blizzards that tapered off, sometimes in seconds.

At night, the winds drove the clouds east toward the plains. Sticks and pinecones rolled across the juvenile center's playing fields, swirling under yellow floodlights into graceless spirits. The kids were at dinner and Marshall was in the common room, playing with his Duplo blocks. He was alone except for an attendant, Leslie, who was pushing chairs under tables, picking up cans, and crumpling wrappers. Leslie had been employed at the juvenile center for nearly a decade, but still worked some of the same tasks as the entry-level attendants. He was a large, fleshy man, his belly protruding between shirt buttons. His hips moved with his torso, he had a slight hunchback that added momentum to his stride, and as he shuffled along, his jaw bobbed so that he appeared to be talking to himself.

Leslie crumpled another wrapper, stuffed it in his pocket, then hovered, prodding Marshall's elbow with the tip of his white clog.

"Ready Freddy?" he asked gently, unlike the other attendants who shot orders through lips.

Marshall whispered goodbye to his Duplo house

and put his Playmobil doll Suzy in his pocket. Leslie took Marshall's hand and guided him from the common room. They entered the dining hall and Marshall was bombarded by sounds and smells; the entryway's swinging doors squeaked and groaned, chatter rose and dimmed as he passed the tables, voices lashed the dining hall's ceilings. An oven beeped like a cicada. There was a clatter of plates being stacked, the squeaking of a trolley.

Marshall stuck his fingers in his ears and blinked rapidly, but it did not block the overhead fluorescent light's reflection against the linoleum. The aluminum railings along the cafeteria snatched the light and angled it back in a bewildering brightness. Leslie led Marshall to his seat, toward a table near the wall. He sat reluctantly, guided downward by the attendant's hand.

"Be back in a minute," Leslie said.

Marshall closed his eyes, rocked back and forth, hummed. Leslie returned with a tray and set it down gently. He explained something about the milk, but through the clamor of the dining hall, Marshall heard only broken fragments, scraps of syllables and vowels. On the plate, the chicken-fried steak was sinking into a pile of mashed potatoes. Marshall attempted to grab it with his hands, but Leslie stopped him by inserting a silver fork between his fingers, their reflections captured in the long silver handle.

Every night, just before lights out, the boys of the juvenile center sat in the TV room watching movies or game shows. During this time, Marshall retreated to his Duplo house, playing while lying flat on his side, arm stretched out under his head.

Tonight, in front of his Duplo house, Marshall tied Suzy to a plastic tree using rubber bands. He tightened the binds until Suzy groaned. Eventually, Suzy murmured, her words coming through Marshall's mouth, "I feel better."

He untied her and said, "I knew you would."

Marshall's Duplo house had five rooms. There was a Duplo brick living room with a fireplace, an L-shaped couch, a television, his mother's books, and photos that climbed up the chimney. There was a stereo where his mother could play country or his father metal. There were paintings that he had made over the years, a low bed for his Labrador, Elway, and a perch for Suzy.

The Duplo kitchen was wide, spacious, and colored in a variety of red, pink, and blue. There was a six-burner stove, a breakfast nook filled with knick-knacks, and a refrigerator covered with drawings and photos. On Fridays, the Duplo kitchen smelled of pizza, the cheap frozen kind that he and his father folded then ate like oversized tacos.

To outsiders, Marshall's Duplo house might appear only inches high, but to him, it was spacious and grand, rising thirty or forty feet. There were three rainbow-colored bedrooms. One for his parents. One for him. And one for Suzy. There was a Duplo freezer, fishing rods, sports equipment, and boxes piled high for Suzy to play in. There was the permanent stain of fingers against the paneling, the grooves of chairs scraped into the floor-boards, the muffled thrum of a dishwasher. There was the dim gray closet nook where dust gathered and clothes hung like shadowy flags, the familiar indentations in the couch cushions, the bed creaking with his weight, and the rafters groaning when the cold fronts drifted in from the north.

When the television was turned off, the kids became restless. Packs of boys roamed, pushing younger kids, spoiling for reactions. These boys had lived in juvenile centers for most of their lives, had learned to circumvent the rules, and preyed on other kids for fun.

A group of boys approached Marshall, one of them muttered a curse, and a current of laughter coursed through their pecking order. They hovered, forming a wall of appendages.

"*Woodchuck*," a boy said.

"*Charcoal*," said another.

"*Get eggs*," another boy snapped.

There was a lull, then movement. A giant foot came down on the back lawn of his Duplo house. Next, a blue sock appeared, crushing the orange roof. The windows and chimneys exploded, scattering his house in all directions.

Marshall wrapped a protective arm around what was left of his house, but a boy's foot in a red sock came down upon his wrist, crushing tendons, veins, and arteries. One of the boys tripped, toppled, and landed on loose bricks. The other boys roared, shoulders bunched together, nostrils, ears, and mouths forming a dark, undulating mass.

***

The isolation room smelled of ammonia and lemon cleaner, foam cushion. There were variations of light, slivers of luminescence appearing through the cracks. There were the sounds of the center's personnel passing, a crackling as the electric kettle in the kitchen boiled to life.

Marshall's head throbbed; his jaw was sore from

the boy's kicks to his face. The bruises on his neck, where the attendants had pried him away, throbbed. He twisted about, chewed on the hard plastic wrist cuffs. He kicked at the door until he could no longer feel his feet, punched at the wall until his fists were bloody.

The smashed Duplo house hovered in his thoughts: sections of walls, doors, and roof scattered across the juvenile center's floor, his home destroyed. Marshall slammed his head against the door. The pain curled then flitted upward. Tears rushed, thick and heavy.

He was touched by a small plastic hand. It was Suzy. She spoke to him through his bruised lips, sounding like Marshall, her voice prepubescent, boyish, a few octaves too high.

The doll stroked the back of Marshall's fingers with her plastic hand. Her mouth was dry like his and he could hear her clearly in his thoughts.

***

At night, the juvenile center was a blend of sounds—a crack of beams, a fluttering of wind against the bay windows. The pine trees creaked deep in their bases, the shifting weather inducing orneriness. Marshall could not be sure how much time had passed since he had been locked up, but he knew it was hours. The other kids had long since gone to bed.

There came a light knock at the door, followed by labored breathing.

Leslie said, "Coming in five."

Marshall closed his eyes, bit at the inside of his bottom lip, muttered, "Five, five, five." He knew one minute was generally a TV commercial break, so he imagined advertisements for cereal, toothpaste, insurance, cars, and pizza. When Leslie slid the lock from its place, the last commercial was finishing up in his imagination, a delivery boy arriving at a family's home with a steaming pizza.

Leslie opened the door, extended his hand from the brightness, the light sticking to his skin and creating a living walkway of muscles and veins. He sat next to Marshall, and their hands brushed one another. Leslie's uniform smelled of sweat and an oatmeal cookie buried in his pocket. His breath emanated machine-made coffee. The plastic cup crinkling in his hands sounded like a cap gun.

Someone flushed a toilet and water moved through the walls, pouring under their feet. Faucets, drains, locks, hinges, creaking beams… In this way, the building was a living being.

"You should be watching television like everyone

else," Leslie said. He touched Marshall's arms, ran his hand over Marshall's cheek. He wheezed out a cough, his lungs clanking as if expelling loose change. He bit at his lip, studying the walls of the isolation room. The attendant started again, speaking slowly, words curling toward a rhythm.

"Kicking they tolerate, punching, yeah, but the biting says that you're an animal. Those boys broke your house. You got to tell yourself, 'So what? It don't matter. I'll build myself a new one.' Instead, you bit one of them to the bone. Fifteen stitches. That other boy, I heard, you went for his eyes. Why you got to do something like that, Marsh? That's enough to get you sent someplace worse than here. You know what will happen in them places, don't you? You'll be sharing a room with four or five others. Kids with no sense. Kids that lost their boundaries."

Using a pocketknife, Leslie cut the plastic cuffs around Marshall's wrists. The lights in the common area had been switched off and whitish-blue strips of light from the alarms floated along the empty tables.

Marshall took Leslie's hand and they walked slowly through the common area, down the hallway, and into Marshall's bedroom. Leslie helped him from his clothes and into his pajamas. In the small sink, he brushed Marshall's teeth, aiming for the molars first, then scrubbing the incisors. The whole time, Marshall closed his eyes and held his mouth open.

When Leslie finished, he rubbed his hand through Marshall's hair and helped him into bed, tucking the sheets and blankets under his arms. Leslie sat down on the end and continued to gaze at Marshall, his face wrenched with restraint. When he finally turned off the light, he remained sitting, waiting for Marshall to fall asleep.

II

Jace opened his eyes and for a brief moment could not remember where he was.

At his feet, Elway stirred. The yellow Labrador was lying near the tent entrance, just at the edge of Jace's mat, his body curled so that his nose nestled into the tip of his tail. The dog was breathing dramatic breaths, as if in deep sleep, but one eye was half-open, monitoring Jace and giving away the act. It was a tradition in their family to name dogs after quarterbacks, and Marshall had named this Lab Elway.

Through the side-slit of the tent, the light of dawn spread into the darkness. The trees were lined with a faint silver. The clouds wavered against the peaks so that the exposed granite appeared to be crumbling. His shoulder winked hot sparks, his neck had a crimp, there was a pine-cone lodged under his arm. Over the course of the night, he had rolled off his sleeping pad.

To his left, Ozzie was snoring through a cold's congestion. A mass of tight, black curls swam against a tide of green Gore-Tex, a white film around the edge of his mouth. Below his eye was a hairless, slug-like scar where, in fourth grade, he had fallen in a rocky stream and Jace had lifted him out, bloody and shocked.

Making as little noise as possible, Jace pulled himself from his sleeping bag, put on his jacket and shoes, grabbed his medical bag, and clambered outside. The wind hit him with frozen, resistant flakes. He studied the cumulus clouds, scanning for hints as to the severity of the oncoming storm. Elway leapt clumsily from the tent and bounded through the snow. As the dog headed toward a distant cluster of aspen, he was snagged by a scent.

There was movement in the next tent over, slow unzipping, cloth sliding against cloth. Jace heard Tamara breathing, raspy and tight, lungs struggling with the altitude. He leaned into her tent.

"You up?"

"Give me a minute," she said.

An icicle dangled above her tent, maybe ten inches away, the water subjected to nature's Bessemer process, sharpened then suffused with bubbles. When it caught the morning light, the ice trapped the illumination and the imperfections shined into being.

Jace trudged to the trees, found a quiet place, out of earshot, and relieved himself. He then hiked to a nearby rock hunkering under a thick cloak of snow and cleared a spot. The forest was heavy with winter silence, a stillness that was bulky and languid. He closed his eyes and sorted through the winter sounds: a creaking pine, the chirp of an early rising chipmunk, the chittering of snowflakes against pine needles.

***

Tamara's tent smelled sweat-damp, a body fighting infection. Her face was puffy, her lips crusted with sleep, her green eyes foggy but alert, like the gaze of a weary mother daydreaming as her baby sleeps. She was a petite woman with tight sinewy muscles and an athletic build. Her physique and ruby skin suggested she had been climbing outdoors for years, but her thighs and shoulders were defined and shaped by the indoors—yoga and Pilates.

"How you two snore," she said.

Jace crossed his legs and asked to see her arm. She removed her fleece jacket, exposing a sports bra. The flash of skin and the intimate space of the tent gave him an unexpected pang.

He recorded her breathing, checked her pulse and temperature, scanned her eyes. He held her arm by the wrist and elbow. Her bruises ran deep, blood seeping from the fractures. His hands went to her shins, pushing her pant legs to expose bruises from her fall, which had spread out in all directions.

Jace let go of her leg, took out a pack of chew, and tucked a pinch in his lip. Tamara straightened her face like most health-conscious people did when confronted with his habit. Chew helped him buzz through stubborn mornings, scattered tantrums, showers where Marshall fought back, hours on the phone with the insurance companies, washing dishes or folding endless loads of laundry.

"You want some water?" he asked. "Apple? Energy bar? Coffee?"

She shook her head. Tamara was thinking about something else, eyes casting about the tent.

"I got a bag full of painkillers," he said. "There's Demerol. OxyContin. Or morphine. Morphine's heavy though."

"Which one do you like?" she asked.

"*Like?*" he thought, irritated by her suggestion.

He handed her an OxyContin and a canteen of water. She swallowed it quickly and, as she drank, her eyes wandered, following her own internal concerns.

"We can try heading out in an hour," he said, rising to his knees.

Something about her look told him she didn't want him there, but she also didn't want him to leave. When she cast her eyes downward, he closed his medical bag, unzipped the tent flap, and stepped out into the snow.

***

Elway came into view, a hundred feet or so up the mountain, sniffing his way across a clearing. The dog's blond body complimented the snowy background, a cream smudge against a monochrome backdrop.

He followed the dog's path until he came to where the dog was attempting to dig out a rodent. Elway stopped and growled every so often, then resumed his frenzy, his nails striking rock. The yellow and orange tents below were animated by the somberness of the gray, stormy morning. They reminded him of a photographic exhibit he and Lynne had seen at a small gallery in Durango while waiting during one of Marshall's therapy sessions. The photographs had been taken on the mountain in black and white, with subjects colored in. A monochrome field with a deer stenciled neon blue.

What Jace remembered the most about the photos was how Lynne had held his hand the entire time. Afterward, they sat in a café across the street, shared an apple muffin, and drank coffee.

"We should do more of this," Lynne said.

Should. A word that buoyed hope.

Jace turned his boot into a drift and spit in the snow, creating a deep brown well. From far away there came the stretched groan of an avalanche.

***

Ozzie had already lit the gas burner and was boiling a pot of coffee. Steam was rising, dispersing through the top mesh, melting an icicle above, a small drip swelling on its tip.

"Visibility's getting worse," Jace said, entering the tent and setting his boots outside. "Checked on *her*. Doing better than I thought."

Ozzie wiped the sleep from his eyes, rubbing hard with the pit of his hand. In the morning light, the loose skin of middle age hung from his chin. Jace still saw Ozzie as his boyhood friend and therefore his true age was always, quietly, startling. Ozzie poured coffee and set the pot down. It was Jace's father's pot, a tin percolator where the clear plastic top indicated when the coffee was dark enough to drink. As a kid, Jace stared at his father who, in turn, stared meditatively at the transparent knob, waiting for that first gurgle of coffee.

"Helicopter?" Ozzie asked.

Jace shrugged his left shoulder as if he had an itch.

"Let's walk it then," Ozzie said and Jace flexed his lips in agreement.

A hard wind pushed the tent sideways, pelting the shell with ice. Ozzie grimaced, the allure of his bright eyes dampened by the wildness of his beard. He cleared his throat and the movement of his Adam's apple lifted his facial hairs like kelp riding a surf.

The snow was moving, cutting across the mountain. A robin bounced from a tree branch and took to the air. They watched it through the tent screen, as if it were part of the storm.

***

They followed the southern face of the mountain, where the grade was gentle and the sled carrying Tamara slipped along smoothly. Many of the wide streams were defrosting, even under a fresh blanket of snow. Water seeped into their boots' eyelets or shimmied between the rubber sole and the leather. Occasionally, they sunk to their ankles in mud. When they pulled their boots out, the black, rotting earth clung to the knobby soles.

The clouds fired flakes through downward currents, pelting Jace and Ozzie's backs until the trail zigzagged through a protective net of aspens, thick white trees sprouting from drifts, stretching to the gray sky. Ozzie led, propping the sled's flexible aluminum brace against his waist while Jace held a plastic rope handle attached to the back. The technique was awkward, clumsy, but worked well if there was a good rapport between the handlers. They had wrapped Tamara tightly, her nose and mouth the only human reference among the blue and orange polyurethane covers.

After hiking nearly five hours, they found a dry spot under a large rock encircled by leaning pines. They pulled Tamara close, fed her, and together they ate wearily, alarmed by the rapid accumulation of snow. Ozzie's beard was white with frost and his yellow goggles gave him the look of a dystopian warrior.

Jace finished his sesame-seed bar, drank half his canteen, took out his tin, and packed his lip with chew. The kick was more disorientating than refreshing.

They set off again, making their way carefully along

the edge of a ridge. For the first time, Jace found himself gasping for air. Sweat was winding down his back.

They followed a trail that sunk slightly into the mountain and the sled seemed to move of its own accord, slipping along the side of the mountain as if propelled by an unseen force. The sound of their boots compacting the snow echoed through the thin pine cover. A crow called out and created a warm solace to their trek, the preceding windy bleakness cloaked by life and the living.

***

Jace and Ozzie were supposed to radio in an update, but the canyon had slowed their progress. Their side of the mountain was lined with dozens of tall, rocky fin-like outcroppings called the Dorsals that blocked radio reception.

They opted for a different route, one that added two hours to the overall trip, but would allow them to radio in when they stopped. They traversed the mountain sideways, slightly uphill, and came to a wide strip of stones blanketing the north slope. There were no trees. Every winter the saplings were flattened and crushed under avalanches.

Ozzie pointed at an orange fluorescent X that had been sprayed onto an exposed rock. Militia groups had been putting out flags like this. Jace and Ozzie had attended to their injured—a broken leg, a gunshot wound, a flare accidentally discharged.

"We got to stop," Tamara said suddenly. "I thought I could hold it, but I can't."

Jace yelled to Ozzie. They set down the sled, unlatched Tamara, put her arms around their shoulders, and carried her over to a distant log. They cleared off the snow and set her down, leaning her back against a rock. It was a pretty good makeshift toilet. Jace handed her wet wipes and she took them sullenly.

As they waited at a distance, backs to her, Ozzie took out a granola bar and split it with Jace. Between crunches, they savored the mountain silence, their bodies vibrating from the exertion.

III

When Marshall awoke, the light angled across his bed, sparking the dust. Out the window, only a few miles away, "The Mountain" was enveloped by clouds.

His father told him that Spanish explorers came this far north, to southern Colorado, and had named the two adjacent mountain ranges, the San Juans and the Sangre de Cristos, respectively. However, "The Mountain" was part of neither range, but a lone volcano that sat between both.

Marshall flopped in his bed, turning away from the window, held his breath, shook his head from side to side, and exhaled through pursed lips.

There was a light knock on the door.

Marshall clambered out of bed, feeling as if he were an oak plank floating upon a foamy tide. When he opened his eyes the ground swayed. He clamped his eyes closed, plugged his ears, snatched at the clothes in his drawers.

He dragged his pants and shirt on, patted his body with his hands, pushed himself to his feet, stumbled toward the door. Remembering Suzy, he called out her name, rushed to the bed, patted it down, ran his hand under the pillow, and found her wedged between the mattress and the bed frame.

There was another knock on the door, one determined strike of knuckles against wood. He stepped into the hallway and an attendant emerged from an adjacent room and blocked him. The strange man's lips and cheeks were chapped and sunburned, shreds of skin peeling away. His eyes were olives behind thick glasses.

"How many times we gotta knock?" he asked.

"One," Marshall said, because it was the only number he could remember.

"Don't you be a smart-ass," the attendant said, thin lips stretching into thin cheeks.

Marshall steered himself around the man, gripping the railing, but was crippled by sharp pins in his feet. His shoes were on the wrong feet. His clothes were inside out. But he couldn't stop or the attendant would come after him.

He weaved down the hallway and made it to the dining hall. He peeked in and looked for Leslie, but through the fuzz of the crowd and the sounds and blinding lights, his equilibrium tottered.

As Marshall entered the dining hall, he turned this way and that, trying to orient himself. Suzy pinched his elbow with her plastic hands, ordered him to go to the other end of the hall. He followed the steel railing, grabbed some silverware and a dish, and drifted toward the food line. A man serving potatoes ordered him to get a tray. When he turned around, another boy brushed past, and they knocked elbows. Marshall dropped his dish and it shattered into two moonlike pieces. One of the attendants jabbed his finger and barked, "*The bathtub is a mean cat.*"

Marshall knew bathtubs were not cats, but before he could ask the attendant for clarification, a second attendant, a woman, began talking excitedly, asking Marshall the kind of questions that were not questions, but accusations ending in a question mark. The grating tone of their voices made him squeamish and he put his hands over his ears. The female attendant yanked them down, splotches of red appearing on her neck. She was shouting indecipherable words, *puts* and *tuts* and *shlluppp*. Marshall pressed against the wall, trying to hide between the bricks.

***

The director was a bearded man with sympathetic eyes. He walked the halls with a modicum of authority, but avoided the boys when they roamed in packs.

Marshall knew the director's name, had repeated it many times, but now, it was lost. He searched the tidy office for a clue. There was a photo of three dogs, blue ribbons hanging on the wall, a rubber tree fading in a corner. He closed his eyes and dug for a visual association.

"*Shrink them purple?*" the director said.

Marshall did not know how to answer the question. He was not even sure if it was a question at all. He wanted to please the director, but he did not want to say the wrong thing so he scrunched his forehead and pretended to think of a response.

"You hear me?"

"Why?" Marshall asked.

The director stared at him with the kind of calm expression that could easily tip into anger. The office was narrow and the walls constricting. When the director leaned back, his chair groaned. When he leaned forward, it chirped. The fluorescent lights roared. In between Marshall's ear and his brain the director's words tightened into a cube and the sentences hurled through context.

"*Making changes near the front,*" the director said, then concluded with, "*Even flies will be getting stuck.*"

Marshall nodded enthusiastically, praying that this was the right response. The gesture seemed to work because the director stood and held out his arms. Marshall stepped forward, but when the director grabbed him tight, he was suffocated by the constricting embrace and the smells of menthol cigarettes, crusted sweat, and coffee. He closed his eyes and fought back one of the two beasts that resided inside himself, the Panic.

***

Marshall had a song that he sang to help him focus. He knew the words, but not the meaning, the melody clinging like spools of spider webs. He sang the song through gym, into lunch, through the afternoon and into dinner, stringing the lyrics front to end in one continuous loop.

Najeneun ttasaroun inganjeogin yeoja
Keopi hanjanui yeoyureul aneun pumgyeok inneun yeoja
Bami omyeon simjangi tteugeowojineun yeoja

Keopi sikgido jeone wonsyat ttaerineun sanai
Bami omyeon simjangi teojyeobeorineun sanai

Geureon sanai

Areumdawo sarangseureowo
Geurae neo hey! geurae baro neo hey!
Areumdawo sarangseureowo
Geurae neo hey! geurae baro neo hey!
Jigeumbuteo gal dekkaji gabolkka
Oppa Gangnam style
Gangnam style

Op, op, op, op
Oppa Gangnam style
Gangnam style

***

After dinner, the attendants put on a movie and went outside to smoke cigarettes. The kids gathered by the television. Lecia, an attendant who did not smoke, who called all the kids sugar, as if they were white blocks waiting to be dropped into coffee, noticed that Marshall was sitting by himself.

"You don't want to watch the movie?" she asked, her neon-pink lipstick cracking into slivers of real-pink skin.

She handed Marshall the box of Duplos, and he scurried to a quiet corner. Lecia hung at a distance, but after a while approached and set a cup of red punch next to him.

"*Crab legs are fine?*" she asked.

Marshall did not answer. He did not even shake his head. She had asked something very different than what he had heard, but he did not want to ask her to repeat it.

Lecia patted the top of his head and walked away, the balls of her shoes squawking as they connected with the linoleum. Marshall lay down on his side, opened the box, began building the Duplo living room. He walled off Suzy's bedroom, constructed her bed from Legos, and then laid the doll down. He combed through the Duplo box with his hands, searching for the right pieces, the rattle of plastic echoing through the common room. A few of the kids, watching television, shushed and cursed at him.

When he finished building his Duplo house, Marshall waited for his mother and father to come home. His mother appeared first, in the Duplo kitchen, standing over a green pot, cooking a split pea soup, something she did in winter, when entire days were freed up due to school and road closings. Every so often, she would glance over her shoulder and smile, as if reminded of some nagging concern. Elway was curled by the fire, his nose pointed toward the kitchen fan. His father was sitting in the next room paying bills, chewing tobacco then spitting into an empty beer bottle.

When he was finished with the house, Marshall tied Suzy to a plastic tree with a piece of birthday ribbon. As he pulled it tight, Suzy gasped and held her breath. The pressure of the ribbon against the doll's body returned her to a calmer state. When he released the ribbon, Suzy leaned against the plastic tree as if she didn't want the experience to end. He grabbed her and held the doll tightly, speaking directly into her ear, much as his father did after tying Marshall to the tree in their backyard.

The movie ended and the television was turned off. The kids sat at tables or circled the floor, and an eerie restlessness descended over the common room. A boy stepped on a plastic cup, lifting his foot up and down so that it crinkled and popped. Someone else tapped a spoon against a radiator; the *tink, tink* was like a pile driver. The boy he bit yesterday lingered a few feet away, jostling and wrestling with a group. They drifted in Marshall's direction.

One boy threw a wrapper at Marshall. Another kicked his leg. The boys condensed into a pack. Marshall's body clenched.

A boy kicked Marshall's hand and Suzy went spinning across the floor and under a radiator. Marshall tried to jump to his feet to get Suzy, but another boy grabbed his ankle and he fell on his face. The boys kicked his house, shattering the windows and walls.

Lecia was writing on the whiteboard and hollered that she was "*crunching over.*"

The Fury was awakening inside Marshall, stretching its wings. It roared and a streak of heat flashed across the surface of his skin. It flapped its enormous wings, squalling like a siren, its reptilian body spreading, fitting into his arms, stretching into his legs.

"*Ignore them yogurt peanuts,*" Lecia said.

"*Trombones for your diet,*" a voice on the intercom said.

"Don't bite," he heard Suzy whisper.

Marshall growled, arched his back, ground his teeth together.

"*You a nibble-babbit?*" the boy who had destroyed his house yesterday said.

Lecia was approaching, fists swinging at the ends of her arms. The boys were looking at her menacingly. One boy threw a Duplo brick at Marshall and it hit him in the back.

Marshall sensed that the pack had decided to attack. He jumped to his feet, spread his arms wide, and howled a dragon's howl. The boys laughed, their tone brittle with anxiety.

"*Crayfish crazy,*" a boy said.

The Fury was surging, the talons on its wings piercing through Marshall's skin, fangs breaking through his gums. The Fury locked eyes with the strongest boy, rose, and snapped its beak. Marshall leapt into the air and sunk his teeth into the boy's neck.

***

Marshall's whole body trembled in panic. A swell in his gut rose. He banged on the door of the isolation room, but when no one came, he defecated right there. He hovered above his mess, picked it up, and, in anger and frustration over his situation, threw it at the bare plywood walls.

"Marsh?" Leslie called out.

Marshall screamed and Leslie threw open the door, his lips flattened, his brows sagged, and he bit through a whimper, as if some internal fundament collapsed. He reached into the isolation room, offering his hand. At first, Marshall didn't move. Leslie waited, breathing through his mouth.

"Suzy," Marshall said and pointed his finger across the room and toward the radiator.

Leslie fetched the doll and when he returned, Marshall snatched Suzy and held the doll close to his mouth, whispering to her.

Gradually, Marshall took the attendant's hand and followed him to the showers. Leslie flipped the tap and water steamed onto the faded turquoise tiles. Leslie rolled his sleeves, soaped Marshall, dried him, led him to his room, and laid out sweatpants and a T-shirt. He placed a first-aid case upon the sheet, popped open the plastic clasps, and took his time opening antiseptics and unwrapping Band-Aids. As he attended to Marshall, he hummed softly, running his hands over the boy's arms and back, examining each wound carefully.

Every so often, he ran his hand through the boy's hair. He set the kit down, huffed as he wiped his nose with the back of his hand. He collected the Band-Aid wrappers with his big, crooked fingers, then scraped the stiff cotton sheet.

"Got you good this time," Leslie said. "Tell me you're okay."

Marshall bobbed his head one time. Leslie's eyes retreated into his heavy brows. The ventilation rattled through the juvenile center, the fresh air being pumped over the white particle board and under the stark fluorescent lights. Leslie put his arm around Marshall and pulled him close. Hugs were overwhelming to his senses, but he did not want to upset Leslie, so Marshall closed his eyes, gritted his teeth, and waited for the embrace to end. When Leslie finally let go, their eyes met and Marshall smiled, but Leslie saw past the expression.

"One day, a long time ago," Leslie said, "when they decided to turn the mountain into a state park, they first had to kick off everyone living on the mountain. Most relocated to towns or just outside the county, but there were a few who stayed on. Supposedly, there was this one boy that no one could control. His mom tied him up in the kitchen, where she could keep an eye on him. The state told her they were going to put him in an institution. She refused. They came for him anyway. So she left the boy in a cave near Fisher Peak. Thought her son had a better chance of surviving in the wild than in an institution. He grew up fine. People saw him every so often. Roaming as if he owned the mountain. Once they even arrested him during a bad winter. He was breaking in to a grocery store at night. They tried to talk to him, but he wouldn't speak. The sheriff thought he was deaf. Maybe he never learned to talk though. No one knows. He started freaking out about the sounds and the noise in the jail. They felt sorry for him and let him go."

Leslie closed up the first-aid box, stuffed the

crumpled Band-Aid wrappers in his shirt pocket. He put his hand to Marshall's forehead and slid the hair from his eyes. "When we was younger we'd go looking for him. Never found him though. There were times I was sure he'd seen us. Someone said he was like the great mountain man, John Colter. That's how he got the name Kid Colter."

Leslie looked outside, at the snow coating the trees. "The water pump's froze again."

Marshall nodded vigorously, grabbed Leslie's hand, and held tight.

"Okay then." Leslie smiled.

***

The van was unsteady in the thick snow. The brakes squealed, worn tires crunched or spun out, all while the radio static of a basketball game ricocheted between bare roof and cracked rubber flooring. The blowers were coughing warm air. Marshall didn't like the passenger seat with the wide, disorienting space between himself and the front window.

They headed along a single road cutting north through a lumpy valley where the elevation was lower and the winds gentler. Eventually, the road narrowed and wound up the mountain. Leslie hunkered in his seat, kept the gear ratio low, licked his lips, and fidgeted with the wipers, matching the steel arm's cadence with the rushing snowflakes.

The snow was deep enough to brush and grind against the undercarriage. The flakes raced through the light cast by the headlights, melting on the windshield. The frozen rubber of the wipers squawked, mirroring the disquiet of the storm.

The snow was getting deeper and every so often, the van fishtailed. As they passed over a cattle guard, something massive and agile roared past the headlights. Marshall saw tangled antlers, eyes, a black snout. Leslie pounded the brakes. The van slid. The beast's enormous, fuzzy rack scraped along the passenger-side window. The van swerved and the headlights flashed over the terrain, disco-lighting the flat, white landscape. The stag flipped one hundred eighty degrees then bounded into the darkness.

Leslie clambered out and studied the situation, leaving the door open, cold, fresh air mixing with the stale warmth of the heater. He looked about, the headlights whitening his face, then let out a laugh that sounded like a hallelujah.

The river to the right lost its wide path while the van was forced into a narrow space between two cliffs and the headlights cast illuminated pods onto the monochrome landscape. The road markings were buried and the edge of the road blurred under drifts. When their tires hit a submerged rock, the truck slid sideways.

After half an hour, they stopped at a clearing. The van's bumper snowplowed, scattering drifts. The chassis settled into the powder, sizzling against the bottom of the engine. They listened to the rattle of the frozen water pump coming from inside a windowless hut, just at the edge of the trees.

Leslie drew a pouch of tobacco and a pack of rolling papers from his jacket pocket. He set his left foot against the steering column, and spun together a cigarette in the same contemplative way that he stirred coffee. Marshall's father had a similar manner when he worked his chewing tobacco, finger kneading the shredded leaves as if fine-motor skills were necessary to the ritual.

He turned his big frame in the seat, springs groaning, and said, "If you're cold, there should be some blankets in with all that camping stuff. I bet you'll even find some snacks."

Marshall leaned over, digging around through the back seats. The juvenile center's vans were used for storage and were full of tents, sleeping bags, ground rolls, flashlights, toilet paper, and boxes of nonperishable food. He pulled out a black sleeping bag and covered himself.

Leslie rolled himself another cigarette. He was smoking slowly, pondering each exhalation and checking the rearview mirror. Eventually, he rolled down his window, flicked his cigarette into the storm, started the engine. He got out, went inside the hut, and was gone for about ten minutes. When he finished defrosting the pump, he climbed back into the van and backed onto the road.

***

The snow was so thick that even the guardrail along the cliff was little more than a hump. As they descended, heading back toward the juvenile center, Leslie sat up in his seat, pressing his face close to the glass. When he pressed the brakes, the van slid and he was forced to jam the transmission into first gear to control their momentum.

The scrape of the windshield wiper and the perpetual squall of the brakes was hypnotic. Marshall's eyes closed on themselves and he nodded off. When the van slid, he bumped his head against the aluminum, opened his eyes, and saw Leslie sitting stiffly, face pressed close to the windshield. Marshall lay down on the back seat.

The dream came immediately. His mother's face was pinched with angst. Marshall was holding shards of glass in his hand and she was asking for them. He wouldn't give them to her. His mother grabbed his wrists, and he bit her knuckles. She slapped him and screamed, "Why are you like this?"

It was a dark and cold dream, one that he had often and that left his body tingling with regret. There were so many memories like this that resurfaced in his sleep, sometimes recast in a hard light, other times jumbled with anxieties.

Coming from beyond his dream, he heard Leslie's voice. The real world was entering, colliding. Darkness was lifting.

Marshall sat up. The van's bumper was scraping dirt. The axle was grinding into the edge of the cliff. The wheels slid, plowing the earth. The headlights slashed space, then flickered to nothing. The van lifted upward, as if it were growing legs. They were upside down, right side up, then upside down again. The dashboard expanded, contracted, and exploded into pellets. The roof bent like a cotton sheet blowing onto a flowerbed, each peak and ridge of varying textures drifting through an undulating space. The windows shattered, almost simultaneously, and in the rear, they flexed, crumpled, bowed, then popped.

Over and over the van tumbled, each and every well-packed thing, with every rotation, coming a little more undone, fracturing, dispersing. They were spinning, sledding, shedding taillights, headlamps, side-view mirrors, snapping trees, shooting down the mountain.

IV

Night came faster than expected, a tangled, gray web cast upon the snow-weighted pines. They could not camp on the cliff because it was too windy, so they cleared a place in the trees, set up the tents, and lifted Tamara from the sled. She was ruffled, but calm, and when she looked back at the mountain, was surprised that they had come so far, so quickly.

After camp was prepared, Jace took his time gathering firewood. He wandered about the forest, meditating among the snowdrifts. In the distance, he heard Tamara speaking with Ozzie.

It took close to an hour for the fire to build, but when it was ready, Tamara sat and gazed into the flames with resignation. Jace set a kettle on the fresh embers. Ozzie said that he was going to hike up a ways and radio in. He tied on snowshoes and took the radio from the sled, setting it into a backpack.

"You from Denver?" Jace asked.

"Born and raised," she said.

"Like it here?"

"I was a partner in a law firm, burning the candle at both ends."

"It's slow enough here."

Tamara smiled a nice smile, moderated by thin lips ringed with wrinkle helixes. "I don't always climb alone," she said.

"You don't free climb a lot either, do you?" he asked, smirking.

She gazed at him before offering a faint, crooked smile. With her sleeping bag draped over her shoulders, Tamara was formless in the dark.

Jace got on his knees and lifted a can of tomato soup out of his backpack, popping it open with his knife. Her eyes followed him as he used sticks as tongs to set the can to the side of the fire, atop white embers. When it was boiling, he set it in the snow to cool, eventually handing it to her. She blew away the steam as Jace set another can in the fire.

He stepped into the darkness and returned with wood. When he threw it on the fire, flames rose and Tamara recoiled from the blast, settled into the change. Elway, who had never been fond of fires, stretched and slunk off toward the tent. The snow was coming sideways, evaporating before striking the fire.

"You don't remember me, do you?" she asked.

He studied her with his usual stoicism.

She added: "Anne Bremmer's office?"

Jace set more branches on the hot coals, then reached into his pocket, pulled out a thin, leather-coated flask of whiskey, unscrewed it. He drank, considering her. She waited and at some point held her palms out as if to say, "You going to answer?"

Jace stood, knees cracking, then abruptly hiked off through the forest without a flashlight. The sound of his breathing rattled through his ears. Soon, he was stepping on logs and snapping branches, crashing his way forward. When the forest broke, a cliff signaled itself with winds gusting straight and unencumbered. Frozen air churned before him, spinning the flakes upward, spitting them back into the storm. The winds against his head were unremitting. He stopped only because he could not go any further. This, in turn, aggravated him, for Jace believed, often wrongly, that movement staved off anger.

***

When he returned half an hour later, Tamara and Ozzie were having a heated conversation. Jace went to the tent, took off his boots, and crawled into his sleeping bag. Ozzie entered the tent, brushed his teeth, then climbed into his sleeping bag.

"You know there's some bad people around here," Ozzie said.

"I don't need any explanation."

"There are kids who need protecting. She was just doing her job. They don't know what you and I know. They saw Marshall as an abused kid."

"I spent the last twelve years fighting for my boy then I got to fight them. I don't know about that woman out there, but Anne Bremmer made me out to be something I'm not. Made other people see it that way too. I'm doing everything to be good and she makes me bad. It's too much to ask of one person."

"It's twelve years out of your thirty-seven."

"Why you got to say something boneheaded like that? You know it ain't over. Marsh isn't any closer to coming home. I'm not strong enough. Don't you get that? I'm breaking here."

"You ain't broken though," Ozzie said. "You said it yourself, years ago, this position you're in…you either keep going or you stop. There ain't much more you can do."

Jace watched his breath rise then hang. The fire outside snapped. Elway was breathing heavily into the side of his sleeping bag.

"I ain't never seen anyone go through what you've had to go through," Ozzie said. "You're right. Of course you're right. It's not fair. Not to you or Marshall. Them taking him like they did. Being the kind of dad you are. Makes me sick. But, I'll tell you this. That boy. You two. You have a connection. A strong one. You hear him like no one else does. You see what no one else does. That bond. It's something special. I don't have that with a single one of my kids." Ozzie paused then pulled the tent flap aside. Tamara had turned off the light in her tent. "It's an unfortunate coincidence that we got stuck bringing her down the mountain, but really, all *she* knows is that you tied Marshall to a tree. Probably read it in the papers like everyone else. Or her colleagues was talking about it, from their perspective. In the end, she didn't talk to you. She don't have no context. She doesn't know why you did it. She sees who you are, now, here. That's what matters."

Ozzie gave Jace the space to respond, but the window came and went. "You know, every night before going to bed, Marisa and I pray for you two. We do. I know you don't like me talking about this kind of stuff. But I'm going to tell you anyway. God gave us faith for a reason, I'm sure.

It carries us through exactly this kind of situation. And you know what else? Marshall will come back. I'm sure of it. God will deliver. You will make it through. I believe it right in my bones, man. I have faith."

"Say Marsh comes home," Jace said. "I can't work and take care of him. Not at the same time. And after he grows up? Then what? I can't take care of that boy for the rest of my life. And even if I do, what does he do when I'm gone?"

"One step at a time," Ozzie said.

"What would happen if I dropped dead right now? Who's going to take care of that boy? God? Let's see how that turns out."

Jace closed his eyes and felt his breath rise above his face then fall back as mist. The temperature was dropping fast, and the world, covered in snow, was freezing in a new way. Ozzie turned out the light. Clumsily, he patted Jace's sleeping bag.

V

The sledding and crashing came to a gradual end. The van was upside down, spinning to a stop on its bent roof. Marshall's body hummed then wakened from shock. He could not feel his arms or his chest. The seatbelt dug into his shoulders.

Marshall pressed the orange button on his seatbelt, using his index finger, then his thumb. He dropped Suzy, watching helplessly as she bounced off the vinyl ceiling. He put more pressure on the orange seatbelt release button, and the metal retainer finally popped. Because he was upside down, he fell hard, stunned, blinked away the static, and patted around the ground until he found the doll.

Marshall shook the door handle. He put his palms against the window frame, popped his head right-side up, and crawled out the opening, toward a pine-needle-coated clearing under a tree.

A thumbnail-size piece of glass was stabbing his right ear. He pulled the shard out, and a dark streak of blood ran down his fingers. He lay down and the snow cooled his cheeks, nose, and forehead. He could feel the cold, but he was not cold.

The van was filling with oil and plastic smoke, twisting and graying against the windows. There was popping, like a firecracker whirling. Marshall was sick with the smells of burning oil, gas, antifreeze; the acrid scents reminding him of an auto garage or butcher shop scrubbed clean.

He crawled back to the van. Leslie was hanging upside down, blood dripping from his mouth. Marshall shook his shoulders. Leslie did not respond. Marshall crawled across the passenger seat, pressed the orange seatbelt button next to the driver's seat. It did not give. Next to Leslie was a piece of metal shaped like an oblong hammer and he used it to pound the seatbelt. As he did this, he sang:

Op, op, op, op
Oppa Gangnam style
Gangnam style

The seatbelt popped, the recoil spooling. Leslie

tumbled onto the roof. Marshall knelt beside him, wrapped his arms around the man's torso. Glass and metal tore Leslie's clothes and skin. Marshall could smell the salt of the man's breath. The attendant was heavy, limp, but inch by inch, Marshall tugged and pulled, gasping and sucking at the freezing night air.

When he pulled the attendant out onto the snow, Marshall paused to catch his breath. He then dragged Leslie to a distant cluster of creaking pines where he was shielded. Leslie's face was splotched with blood, blushed in some places, pale in others, cuts on his arms running so deep that bone and veins were exposed. Leslie's left leg, from the knee down, was little more than ivory splinters protruding through skin.

Marshall ran his fingers over the cool creases in Leslie's flesh, through the thin black body hair, and around the oily bald areas where his hair thinned and withered. There were shards and slivers of glass embedded throughout his skin, shimmering like mica. One of the arteries in Leslie's arm had been cut and blood pumped onto the snow.

Marshall struggled to his feet, trudged to the van, climbed in, and tore away a piece of vinyl from the passenger seat. He returned to Leslie and tied the strip around the man's arm, pulling tightly until the blood from the artery slowed. He retrieved more vinyl, using the pieces to bandage the man's broken leg, his wrist, chest, and leg wounds. He picked out the small pieces of mirror, glass, and plastic, working steadily until he was shivering from the cold.

He lay down on the snow, curled into a fetal position, knees to chest, arms crossed, and watched the van as if it were a dwindling campfire.

***

Someone called to him. There was nothing except the pines, the drifts, and the clouds. The voice came again, shrill and authoritarian.

Marshall looked up and saw Suzy standing just above his forehead. The doll's pen-dotted brown eyes darkened to black, her mouth, usually a half-moon, was a straight line. Her detachable hair was stiff in the breeze, single-line mouth parting into two thin lips. She wrapped her arms around her body and exhaled, her lips extending into a dramatic pucker.

"It must be twenty below," she said, studying the distance.

Suzy was searching for something particular.

"There's something," she said. "You know what? We've been here. Two years ago. I remember. Up the cliff."

The doll jumped into Marshall's pocket and tugged him in the direction she wanted to go. They clambered up a cliff, scaled a ledge, and entered a cave. It was about the size of his bathroom, higher at the entrance than it was long. Warmth from the earth seeped through the cracks in the walls. The cave had veins and arteries, cracks that blued, blackened, then oozed into lichen.

Suzy vanished into the darkness, her plastic feet clicking on the rock.

"It smells like bark," he said.

"Like drying clay," she said.

"Like compost."

"We came up here with your dad," she said.

"I'll go get some stuff. We can sleep here."

"How long will you be?"

"I'll be back in a second."

"One."

"Okay. Three hundred seconds."

The doll started counting, very slowly.

***

Inside the van, Marshall collected two sleeping bags, apples, a bottle of water, a large flashlight, and a headlamp. His sweatpants did not have enough pockets, so he stuffed everything in a plastic bag. He wiggled on a headlamp and cast the LED light upon the ground, dulling the stark white snow.

Dragging the supplies behind him, he returned to Leslie, held his fingers to the attendant's neck. He could not count, but if he sang, a healthy pulse fell neatly within the beat.

Najeneun ttasaroun inganjeogin yeoja
Keopi hanjanui yeoyureul aneun pumgyeok inneun
yeoja
Bami omyeon simjangi tteugeowojineun yeoja
Op, op…

The tempo of Leslie's heartbeat did not match the rhythm of the song. It was too fast. Marshall went around the man's body, first lifting one leg, then another, then both arms. He wiped off the snow gathering on Leslie's chest, sighed, turned away, and clambered up the side of the cliff on all fours. Inside the cave, he unloaded the bags, water, and apples, looked about with his headlamp.

Suzy hadn't moved and Marshall wondered why she

hadn't used the time to unpack or clean.

"I can't carry Leslie," he said.

"How many tons does he weigh?" she asked.

Marshall did not know measurements, especially with weight, so he said the first number that came to mind. "Ten."

"Ten." Suzy nodded, as if this sounded reasonable. "That is a lot. But not impossible. Maybe you're just scared."

"You know I'm not scared of anything," he said.

"You're scared of electric eels," she said. "You're scared of Michael Jackson 'Thriller' zombies."

Marshall closed his eyes and peered through his eyelashes.

"You have to be the Little Engine That Could," Suzy said. "You either 'keep going or you stop.' That's the truth. You have to do it. You can do it. You can pull Leslie up here. You know you can. Look at you. You're not ready to stop."

"I have to keep going."

"And you can," she said with a nod. "I want you to say, 'I'm not going to stop.'"

"I'm not going to stop!"

"Say it again!"

"I'm not going to stop!"

Suzy gave him a shove and he slid from the edge of the cave. The headlamp was flickering, and there were stretches when he couldn't see where he was going, but the smells of pine eventually gave way to diesel, oil, and antifreeze. When he caught the odor of stale cigarette smoke, he knew he had reached Leslie. He knelt, took off his gloves, set his cheek next to Leslie's mouth, and felt a faint, staggered breath.

He wrapped his arms around Leslie's torso and began to pull the attendant's body. Inches became feet. Marshall was wearing a hat, gloves, and a decent winter jacket, but his feet were already tingling. His forehead burned with frozen sweat. Breathing became so painful that he was forced to stop dozens of times, covering his nose and mouth to mitigate the cold. There were times when he was not aware of what he was doing, when the earth and the sky and his thoughts were a single muddy conglomeration.

Marshall's feet sunk into the snow. Several times, rocks and branches crumbled under his weight and he fell onto his back. The ground became so steep that if he let go for even a second, Leslie's body would slide downward.

"I'm not going to stop," he muttered. "The Little Engine That Could. *Op op Gangnam style.*"

VI

When Jace awoke to the purple light of morning, the storm was still pounding the tents, skittering pellets along the polyester shells. He got up, relieved himself in the trees, and afterward stood listening to the snowflakes falling on pine needles. Buried in his pocket was an old packet of chew. He placed some between his lip and gums and crumpled the package. The tobacco was tender, alive in his mouth, sharpening the end of a long, dreary night.

"I'm going to go check in," Jace said to Ozzie through the tent.

Tamara unzipped her tent, and still in her sleeping bag, leaned forward into the morning air. She puffed herself up and scratched her short hair to attention. She was making an effort, trying to apologize through a pleading gaze.

Jace unlatched snowshoes from his pack, worked

the laces, strapped them onto his boots, and, not wanting to meet Tamara's eyes, studied the mountain. There was little to see except the occasional black spots of exposed rocks or the uncovered pine boughs drooping under white piles.

***

It took him awhile to get settled in a windless spot and turn on the radio. When he got through, the connection crackled in a way that seemed to imitate the pattern of the falling snow. Chaz was on dispatch, just about to end his shift.

"I've been trying to get through to you guys. Is the radio off?"

"It's not working at the camp," Jace said.

"The juvenile center called last night. Said Marshall went missing. Sheriff's department is out looking, but this storm is slowing things down. The guy they think took him. His last cell-phone record is ten miles east of the juvenile center. Highway 71 east was closed at the tavern so…"

"What about west?"

"Marker twelve. Where the gate is. A mile before the pass."

"Sounds like they went to the water pump," Jace said. "Was the guy who took him Leslie?"

"That's what I wrote here," Chaz said, then asked, "You know him?"

"He's a good guy. Probably took Marsh out for some fresh air."

"In this storm? Who does that? Listen. You almost down with Tamara?"

"Three hours, give or take."

"Jim's already at the trailhead. We're getting a search party for Marsh together."

"What time they close the roads last night?"

"Early," Chaz said. "Six or seven."

They said goodbye and Jace switched off the radio. He packed up and started to head back to camp, but stumbled and fell to his knees. He stood, but immediately fell again. He forced himself to his feet, stumbled, and out of sheer frustration, rammed his head into a drift. He inhaled and pinched his eyes closed, sucked at loose ice fragments. A scream came first, emanating from his neck. Next came a hard shudder, like an engine seizing. His body heaved and each convulsion wracked his gut. He fell facedown into the snow and cried harder than he had ever cried before.

Eventually, he lifted his face from the snow, sat back

on his knees, and looked into the sky. His knees cracked as the back of his thighs met his calves. The flakes landed on his cheeks and forehead, pricking, melting. He took off his gloves, wiped his face, and reached inside his jacket. The tin was gone, but he could feel tobacco remainders in the corners of the pocket. He plucked the strands of chew with his thumb and forefinger, picked out the lint, and slid the dry shreds of tobacco between his gum and lip. There was not much, but the minor kick made him tear up all over again.

***

By the time Jace returned, Ozzie had packed Tamara and the sled. When Jace told him what Chaz had said over the radio, Ozzie squinted and ran his hand over his mouth, smothering a curse.

"Listen," Jace said. "I'm thinking if I get going, I can be at the pass a little after lunch. If they're not there, I'll follow the road back. Go to the water pump."

"You don't think that's a bit optimistic?"

"Can you bring Tamara down by yourself?"

"It's nothing but flat trail the rest of the way," Ozzie said, wrestling with the strategy.

"Can I have the food?" Jace asked Ozzie as he slung on his backpack. "And that extra medical kit?"

Ozzie stretched his nostrils in disappointment. He went to the sled and returned with the medical kit, a water bottle, three energy bars, and trail mix, handed over the food, but held on to it until Jace looked him in the eyes.

"When the storm's over," Jace said, lowering his tone, "I might need a helicopter…"

Ozzie was struggling to overcome his suspicion and give in to trust. His eyes went cold with the realization that something questionable was unraveling.

"I'll be at the top, between Fishers and Washington Peaks," Jace said, leaning into Ozzie. "Marsh's going to the top of the mountain."

"Why would he do that?" Ozzie asked, but Jace was already packing his bag. "Listen, when I get this gal to the bottom, I'm coming back to find you. Your phone charged?"

"I think it still has some juice," Jace said.

"Take the radio."

Jace looked toward Tamara, who was watching with concern. Ozzie started to speak, but stopped himself.

Jace pressed his lips together and gave Tamara and Ozzie a nod, then trudged off, snowshoes compacting the powder. A minute later, Ozzie shouted something about "faith," but most of the sentence was lost.

***

Clouds obscured the mountain peak and crept along the valley. The temperature was rising and the thin flakes fattened. Until the sun passed its high point, the snow would continue to get thicker and visibility would decrease.

Jace had not eaten enough food, had not slept properly, and his endurance was weighted by worry. However, if he went any slower, it would be night by the time he reached the place where he suspected Leslie and Marshall had gotten stuck with the van.

The elevation was high, the air dry, and dehydration a serious threat, but he drank sparingly from his canteen. Being on the mountain, in a snowstorm, was comparable to being on the sea; water was all around, but drinking came at a price. Heating the snow required fuel while eating it cold cooled a body's core temperature.

He decided to push himself for longer distances, then take long breaks. He set a goal, a clearing not far up the mountain, where there was an old mine, discarded rocks thrust out like a tongue. When he was younger, he could have charged through the exertion, but now he acutely felt his age, his weight, and the degradation stress had caused on his physique and stamina.

Passing the abandoned mine, he hiked along a precipice where the storm surfed the cliff, swirling with such malicious turbulence that if he were not wearing snowshoes, he was sure he would have been blown over.

Jace arrived at a fork. He could either go down a steep incline that ended at a cliff, which he would have to descend without climbing gear. Or, he could climb another precipice a mile south, and afterward hike east.

I have no other choice except to take the cliff, he thought.

He was there in a few minutes and when he stepped toward the edge, he saw that it was not a long climb, but it was too far to jump safely.

Jace zipped his jacket to his chin, tightened the laces on his boots. The cliff face was sheer granite with narrow toeholds. He took the first step. The rock was slippery. His boots were knobby. He gripped a pine root, took another step, lowered himself to the first foothold, and came eye level with the dog.

Elway was studying him, lying in the snow, his body a cream-colored Rorschach. He was panting, a single drop of saliva dangling from the tip of ham-colored tongue.

The dog would find a way down by himself. He knew the trails well.

Jace took another careful step downward, aware of every inch of his own exposure to the void. A gust came from the side, sanding his neck and cheeks with grit.

He counted his steps. One. Two. By the eleventh step he was assured by his own momentum. He found each step and toehold with ease. The rock was cold and the tips of his fingers were becoming numb. He was moving too fast. He knew it. He still had at least two hundred feet to go.

He came to a crack as large as himself, but narrow enough to leverage his body. He pressed one boot against the side and ground his back into the rock. Taking off his left glove, he blew on his bare fingers, then took his right glove off and repeated the process, the warmth causing the tips to sting slightly. He drank from his water.

There were several icicles hanging inches from his face. He thought how Marshall was obsessed with icicles, collecting them with urgency, leaning them against one another vertically, like a teepee, then hoisting packs of fluffy snow minarets atop their points.

Let's keep going, he thought.

The rocks were coated in a single sheen of ice. As he continued to descend, he pressed hard against the rock face, leveraging his weight as efficiently as he could, but at some point it was not enough. It was too slick, his fingers were too cold to grip, and the wind pulled at his body.

Seconds later, he was stepping too far to the right, overextending his left leg. One of his fingers slipped. He overcompensated, clawed at the granite, and his right foot kicked loose what had been a stable hold. He leaned forward, but the movement was too fast. Both of his feet were in the air.

Wind filled his ears. He did not struggle, did not try to right himself.

Why am I not fighting this fall? he thought, before hitting the ground, torso landing in a drift. The impact snapped his head back, striking a snow-covered rock. The thud echoed in his skull.

VII

Marshall slept feverishly and awoke often. In the early dawn, when traces of purple infused the sky, he opened his eyes and saw Suzy standing guard at the edge of the cave.

He spied movement from beyond the cave: sniffing, grunting. He smelled dogs, not like Elway, but wild, unwashed animals, coyotes. He and Suzy listened as they came closer. When they were only a few feet away from the cave's mouth, Marshall flung his sleeping bag aside and yanked on his boots. He stepped from the cave and sniffed the air. A shadow moved just feet away. Another flashed past.

Marshall was not fully awake, but his adrenaline had awoken the Fury. It spread its wings and extended its talons. When another coyote passed at a distance, he charged down the hill, barking and snarling. The coyotes yelped in surprise, fled into the darkness.

Marshall growled, then barked as low and commanding as a St. Bernard. He swore that if they returned, he would kill them.

***

The sun's light presented itself as a clue through the thick clouds. It was six a.m. Marshall knew that for sure. His time was as regular as it was internal. Eight to bed. Six awake.

He sat up, realized that there was no schedule, no breakfast, no gym, no common room time. No social interactions to navigate, no need to speak, no attendant's commands to interpret. His muscles tingled and he jerked around in his sleeping bag, chasing the fleeting itches, then lay back, kicking his legs into the air. The snow came at an angle, lining one side of the pines with thick white powder while leaving the other untouched. There were figures and faces in the flurries, entire topographies blown away with a gust.

Submerged in his sleeping bag, Leslie's chest rose and dropped in a staggering, convulsive repetition. He gasped for air like a catfish in a dry bucket and his breath had the sourness of moldy orange peels.

The bottles of water from the van were near the back of the cave. Marshall retrieved one, broke the seal, poured a capful into Leslie's mouth. His throat convulsed, forcing the water back out and over the sides of his swollen lips.

Suzy was still standing near the cave entrance, the dim morning light concealing her features. She could easily be mistaken for an apple core or a candy-bar wrapper.

"Breakfast," he said to her.

"Who said they were hungry?"

Marshall grabbed Suzy, put on his boots, sweatpants, Leslie's wool hat, a hooded parka, and made his way down to the van. Most of his tracks from the night before had been filled in, but he could still make out faint impressions.

The van itself was covered in a layer of snow. A curtain of icicles grew along the running boards. Snow had settled upon the wreck, concealing tires, axles, and flattening the uneven assemblage of the undercarriage. The burnt and charred smells had congealed into a foul, vagrant odor.

Marshall set Suzy on the ground and crawled into the upside-down van. The ceiling was the floor and the floor the ceiling and this made him giggle for he had once been to a carnival in Walsenburg where there had been a funhouse and the bathroom had been upside down. He had loved that bathroom and refused to leave because it was how the real world often felt.

Reaching around the hanging stick shift, he patted between the floor and the driver's seat. Caught in that small place, where the seat cushion was held in place by a spring, were receipts, an orange lighter with a sketch of a lampshade, gum chewed then rewrapped, straws, toothpicks, coins, a traveler's tube of toothpaste. He almost stepped on the rearview mirror and sunshade, where Leslie kept his sunglasses in a pouch.

The myriad of smells coming from the van triggered a flood of associative memories: the steamed kitchen window when his mother cooked, the plaster cast for a fractured limb, sewer pipes opened at dawn. Suzy wiggled out of his pocket, sniffed, and together they swam in the smells. They were transported to the chicken-frying vat used during church auctions, the thrift store cashier with cheddar halitosis, the blue-lagoon toilet water in the attendants' office that colored green when mixed with urine.

His stomach grumbled. "You came here to eat," he reminded himself.

Next to him were crushed cardboard soup boxes, cans of ravioli, burst juice boxes. Cocoa coated the tents, the toilet paper, sleeping mats, sweet powder moistened then dried into a half-hardened brown enamel. Marshall salvaged a few upturned boxes of juice, grabbed what food he could, went and sat down against a rock, pulled apart a pack of potato chips, and pushed fistfuls into his mouth. He ate ravenously, devouring one chip after another.

As he finished, a heaviness swelled in his abdomen. At first he tried to ignore the pressure, but when it threatened to exit on its own, he went to a distant tree, pulled down his pants, squatted. Crouching, waiting for his body to cleanse itself, he stared into the storm. The snow fell with light *ka-thunk*s. He pointed at the individual flakes and assigned numbers.

"Four, one, twenty, four, two, eight, thirteen."

He closed his eyes, tilted his head back, and thrust out an arced tongue. He made a gurgling sound that balanced his body and mind, imposed an audible order over the unpredictability of nature. When he was finished, he stood and studied his leavings. His feces steamed, smelled like who he was inside, a digestive history. These were the last traces of the juvenile center, the pink tatters of hot dog and tapioca raisins, fried potatoes with corn and onions.

Marshall did not wipe, did not clean his hands. His conscience burned with guilt and his shoulders stiffened as he anticipated his mother scolding him. He fixed his pants and wandered to the river. He stood on the ice. Bubbles traced underneath, scattering from his weight.

He stepped farther and with the edge of his toe, pressed a cracked seam. The sound was a ghostly exhalation, shuddering pines, ripples under the ice.

He looked about. The clouds and the snow now cut visibility to less than a hundred feet. They formed an intimidating phalanx, their force buttressed by the wind.

He took another step onto the ice and it gave, his foot slipping into the shallow water. He pulled it out and a moist chill leaked through his boot's eyelets and against his thin socks. He smiled as the cold and wet seeped along his toes.

***

When he returned to the van, Suzy was waiting in the same place he had left her. They sorted through the camping equipment together. Standing on top of a red plastic container, the doll met his eyes. "We need to make a plan."

"Why?" he asked.

"We can't stay here forever," she said.

"Why not?"

Suzy raised her eyebrows skeptically. Marshall

leaned close to her face, meeting the black dots that were her eyes.

"I wouldn't be missed," he said.

He packed a snowball, threw it against the van.

"If I'm gone," he continued. "If I disappear for good. My dad could do whatever he wants. He could start his life all over again. He wouldn't have bills. He wouldn't worry about the bank taking our house."

"He wouldn't have you," she said.

"We can stay on the mountain and be like Kid Colter."

Suzy exhaled. "If we stay here we'll die. You want to die?"

"Who says we're going to die? My dad taught us everything."

"What if he didn't? What if there's some important thing he forgot? Did you ever think of that? I don't want to take the risk and find out."

"Well, even if we don't stay here," he said, "we need to go to the top of the mountain."

Suzy rolled her eyes dramatically.

"You know," Marshall said, wagging his index finger. "My dad told us. He said that when you die…"

"…*You go to the top of the mountain*," Suzy finished for him. "I know. I was there."

The doll's monochrome color was giving way to a burgundy flush and her black, pinprick eyes were flattening into slits.

"Your dad also told you that you can't just go anytime you want."

"That was because I was mad and he didn't want me to run away."

"If we go to the top of the mountain," she said, "you'll be more lonely than you were at the juvenile center. Lonelier than you were at school, where they kept you in a separate room. Lonelier than when you had to stay at home because none of the schools would take you. At the top of the mountain you'll be the loneliest boy in the world. And you might also be dead."

Suzy stared at him, running her hand over a faint crack in her plastic chest, caused either by the extreme cold or the crash.

"How many times did your mom tell you there aren't sharks in the bathtub," she went on. "How many times has your dad told you that Michael Jackson 'Thriller' zombies aren't real, but you still think they'll attack you in the shower?"

Marshall clicked his tongue against the top of his mouth.

"Look," she said, "your dad's a good man. He told

you that your mom was dead because he wanted to protect you. He made up that ridiculous story that when we die, we go to the top of the mountain. He knew you'd believe it, because it was *so* ridiculous."

"Just because a story is ridiculous doesn't mean I'll believe it," Marshall said.

"Yes it does."

"No it doesn't."

"Shark!" Suzy shouted. Marshall spun around. Suzy laughed, but her pen-line smile and pinprick eyes did not waver. "You spread your mom's ashes. That might have seemed real. But it wasn't. Those ashes were probably from the neighbor's barbecue."

"You don't know that."

"Your mom didn't die."

"Yes she did."

"I was up the night your mom left," Suzy said. "I heard them talking. I saw them through the window, outside. Just before she got in the car and drove off."

Suzy took Marshall's hand in hers, but he pulled it away.

"You heard it too," she said.

Marshall shrugged and lay down on his stomach, pulling his arms over his head. His father told him that when his mother died, she had gone to the top of the mountain. In the back of his mind, he suspected that his mother wasn't really dead. He had read it in the way his father behaved, the hushed conversations with Ozzie, and the sad looks he got from older women in town. Still, he loved the idea of his mother being at the top of the mountain, far above the social workers, the unpaid bills, the endless therapy visits, waiting for him and only for him. He loved the idea that he could be reunited with her and ask for her forgiveness for all the pain he had caused her.

***

Marshall and Suzy decided to build a fire so that search and rescue could find Leslie. Marshall scurried from tree to tree, collecting dry wood. He threw it all into a pile just above the cave, poured gasoline from one of the van's canisters on the wood, tossed on a match, and the kindling exploded. The wood snapped and with each split, there was a chattering as the flames grew higher. He stepped closer, the hair on the back of his hands curling from the heat.

He went to get some more wood and came across a dead sparrow at the base of the tree, its bones and feathers bleached by exposure. The bird's beak was chipped in such a way that it looked like a miniature bullhorn. He moved the bird's skull back and forth, held it up to his nose and sniffed.

Skeleton in hand, Marshall danced around in the snow, singing "Gangnam Style," then fell hard on the ground. The collision with the earth jarred his mind and body. Eventually, he just lay in the snow. He could feel the skeleton in his hand. He had crushed it. When he opened his hand, the pieces of white bone fell and were indiscernible from the snow.

VIII

Jace listened to the chatter of snow blown loose by the wind. He slowly opened his eyes, blinking into a sky of silver and zinc. He sat up and looked about and saw the steady curtain of snow and the mountain peak outlined in the distance. He strained to stand and when he did, his vision blurred. He leaned into the wet cliff face, waiting for the spinning in his head to still. There was a pain in his chest, the pinching throb of cracked bone. One by one, he examined his ribs, applying soft pressure, until he found the bone that was hurting the most. A jolt of pain momentarily dizzied him. He cursed at his stupidity. A broken rib in this weather, on this mountain, could be fatal.

He brushed himself off and surveyed the hillside. The high currents were winding through the canyons, the invisible movement vast and insuppressible. The land sloped into scoliotic pines whose backs were arched and shorn by wind. He heard avalanches near the peaks, a tumbling thread of diverse granulates emptying nearby ridges, reminding him of waterfalls after a heavy summer downpour.

He found his backpack a few feet away. His sunglasses were gone and so was his right snowshoe. He would have to manage the deep snow only in his hiking boots.

Jace whistled, cupped his hands, and called again, hoping his voice would penetrate the thick clouds. Elway must still be at the top of the cliff, Jace guessed, or he was already finding his way back down.

A few hundred feet away there was a white line winding through trees and rock. It was the Yankton trail where, just two years ago, he had hiked with Lynne and Marshall. Marshall had been lagging far behind, muttering to himself and his doll. Lynne had been wearing tight gray jeans, which she tucked into her wool socks and hiking boots. She hadn't shaved for days so the black stubble under her arms was visible with each stride. When they stopped and waited for Marshall, Jace used the time to hold his wife and kiss her sweaty neck.

There were memories seemingly everywhere: a rockslide where, many years earlier, he found his first arrowhead, a knot of trees where he taught Marshall how to read topographic maps. At the bend in the Northfork

River, thrumming like a generator, he had shown Marshall how to clean a pan using shrubbery, how to wash his face, arms, and legs without getting too much water on his clothes, and how to dip their hats so that their heads stayed cool as they hiked. The memories made him choke. He brushed away the tears with the frozen crusted edge of his glove.

***

The lower the elevation, the flatter the slope, the deeper the drifts became. The purled edges of the river came into view, cutting the rocky mountain crags. He saw a gray plume, far in the distance, snaking between the earth and sky.

He took out his binoculars and became convinced that the plume was from a campfire. The smoke might be from hunters or militia, but they rarely came up in the dead of winter and hardly ever during a storm. He lowered the binoculars and walked faster, encouraged. Soon, he was jogging, clambering through the trees and snow, trying to ignore the throbbing in his ribs, but the pain was acute. With each step, he could almost taste blood in his mouth and every so often he stopped, coughed, and hacked pink phlegm.

Twenty minutes later, he stopped and surveyed the clearing. The fire had died considerably. The trees had been blackened, the side of the mountain had melted into muddy channels, and whoever had made the fire had done so with enough skill to ensure that it would smoke for hours.

He leaned against the side of a tree, sweat pouring down his face and neck. He spotted footprints running through the trees and up the side of the mountain. The pieces were coming together, but not fast enough.

The side of the mountain was granite with wide veins of limestone. Over eons, water had dripped through the cracks and the limestone had eroded into caves.

Climbing upward, stopping every so often to call out, Jace recognized an unhealthy rankness in the air. An opening, a few feet wide, appeared. He climbed over, peered in, and discovered a water bottle, apple cores, and a juice box.

There was a sleeping bag, toward the back. He hesitated. A million felonious scenarios played through his mind. He touched the sleeping bag lightly, his heart pounding.

He climbed to the other side of the bag and was morbidly relieved when he saw Leslie's pale face peeking out from the polyester. The inside of the sleeping bag was coated in a black burgundy and there were bits of flesh and hair dried to the polyester lining. Leslie's skin was splotched and marked with deep bruises. One arm was bent so badly that Jace guessed it must be broken in several places. The other had been severed neatly near the joint at the elbow and the stump was a yellowish, crusty mass. The blood flow had been stopped with a vinyl tourniquet and capped with a plastic bag. There were vinyl strips everywhere on his body, applied as makeshift Band-Aids.

It took him several minutes to find Leslie's pulse. It was soft, but the beat was rapid. He dug around in his pack, found a pen flashlight, and shined it in Leslie's eyes. His pupils dilated slowly.

He went to the lip of the cave, cupped his hands around his mouth. "Marshall!" he shouted as loud as he could, unnerved by the alarm in his own voice. He waited, but there was no response. Even if the boy could hear him, Jace wasn't sure he'd shout back. Marshall had never been able to gauge the alarm in another person's voice.

Scanning the valley, Jace saw something that looked like a giant molar. He jogged out of the cave and down the hill, slipping on loose rock. As he got closer, he saw a van. The front and back were contorted inward, aluminum rearranged to almost molecular dimensions. The engine was in the driver's seat, the front passenger seat had been ripped from its mooring, and only one seat-bench in the back remained.

Snowdrifts had accumulated against the sides. Frozen engine fluids left amber and azure icicles along the dashboard. Toward the back, the snow was blowing in sideways, piling upon the roof. There were boxes and backpacks that had been opened after the crash, packages ripped open, backpacks unzipped.

"Marsh!" he shouted, the words falling flat against the silence.

He surveyed the footprints until he found a set that went past the van and through a small crevasse, veered through pines, and eventually disappeared behind a granite rock. He followed them up the mountain, but he stopped. Judging from the accumulated snow and the fire below, he guessed that the footprints were from sometime in the morning.

He scanned the peaks with his binoculars, but the storm was thick and the visibility was low. He called out again and again.

If he could call in a helicopter or a plane, the boy could be found before nightfall. Rio Arriba County had a plane. Peterson Air Force Base sometimes loaned their drone for search and rescue. He cursed himself for leaving the radio with Ozzie. Taking out his phone, he dialed search and rescue dispatch. It rang twice then cut out. He tried again, but the signal was too weak.

***

Jace crouched in the cave, listening to the irregular rise of Leslie's breath, the crackling of the fire, the water dripping. He took out his medical kit, retrieved a small IV bag, pressed around for a vein in the attendant's remaining arm, inserted the needle, and placed the bag on a rocky ledge. He added antibiotics to the IV, stitched Leslie's larger wounds, and, heating the end of his hunter's knife over the coals of the fire, cauterized the arteries and bandaged the stump the best he could.

Afterward, Jace stayed by the fire. Marshall had left a stack of branches, so with little effort Jace got it going again. Building on the coals, it crackled and rose steadily higher into the dusky gray night.

He ate two granola bars, a pair of cold Pop-Tarts, a box of cheese crackers, swallowed two ibuprofen. As evening approached, the temperature dropped rapidly and he was grateful for the low-pressure system that brought cloud cover with it. A clear night would have been much colder and even more dangerous for Marshall.

He watched the snow spin through the dark, hazy evening. The last light haloed the mountain, cement-gray clouds chipping into white, flaky pebbles. Each snap of the fire was made distinct by the lull that followed.

It made him nauseous and weary to think of Marshall by himself, in the cold night. He hated the idea. Hated that he could not protect his son, even if the danger originated with his own stupid lie.

I never should have told him his mother was at the top of the mountain, he thought.

Every so often, Jace returned to the cave to check Leslie's pulse. The IV was helping. The attendant's eyelids fluttered occasionally and he muttered incoherently.

Jace picked up an apple stem lying next to the sleeping bag. It was Marshall's, he was sure. The boy devoured apples. Jace lay down on the cold rock, on his good side.

His ribs throbbed like burning splinters. Hot and cold sweats came and passed. He swallowed three more ibuprofen.

Using his compass to give approximate coordinates of the canyon, he composed a text of his location, pressed send, and waited. Almost a minute later he saw the "received" notification.

Jace sipped his water, and waited for a reply. The

phone's signal flickered from one bar to none then back to one bar. He tried another message, typing the letters with cold fingers. "*Going up to the pass.*" When he hit send, the transmission bar reached the end, the signal died, and there was no confirmation that it had been received.

IX

Marshall had been hiking with Suzy for most of the day through the forest. The snowflakes came straight down, as if the clouds were shedding. The wispy thin trees slowly gave way to a long, flat-white meadow where boulders wore powdery skullcaps.

The soaring mountain peaks were three beings of sheer granite, each hundreds of feet tall, striking the sky defiantly. Their names came from the Zuni Indian kachinas: *Uhepono*—a hairy underworld giant; *Achiyalatopa*—a powerful monster whose feathers were flint knives; and *Amitolane*—a giant rainbow spirit. Marshall had once seen the kachina dolls in a shop and been hypnotized by their colors, their solid, wild eyes, and the ferocity of their gaze.

He was carrying a daypack stuffed with supplies culled from the van: a sleeping bag, a lighter, juice boxes, granola bars, spicy jerky sticks, and a change of clothes.

Suzy led from Marshall's shirt pocket, ordering him to turn this way or that.

They passed through a narrow passageway that he imagined was the entrance of a gigantic maze. He hummed "Gangnam Style," but in a low, eerie tone. He often stopped and gazed into the sky, squinting, blinking, infusing his eyes with light; like Morse code, each break, each flash of sun between blinks was its own secret meaning.

Even though the snow had been falling heavily for hours, the depth of the snowpack remained consistent. However, in some places the top layer was frozen and could support his weight while in others, it broke and he sunk up to his knees. He was still going too slowly for her, trudging along, carrying a dozen fist-sized rocks. Marshall had always liked to carry exceptionally heavy things so that he could feel his body in relation to the earth. When he had attended school, he carried around textbooks and dictionaries. At his physical therapy appointments, he lifted the weighted balls. In the backyard, he often moved bricks and cement blocks from one side to the other and back again.

"I'm tired," he said.

"Ditch the rocks."

"Can I ask you a question?"

"Does it have to do with being tired because you're carrying rocks?" she asked.

"Where are we going?"

"We're going to the top of the mountain because that's what you want," she said.

"Right," Marshall said. He hesitated before asking the next question because he knew it would tap her annoyance. "Why?"

"'Why?'" she huffed. "Are you seriously asking me that? Do you really not know the answer or are you just asking 'why?'"

"Why?"

Suzy pinched his left cheek, right below his eye.

"My mom," he said quickly. "She's at the top of the mountain waiting for us. That's why."

"Right. Because that's what you think. You think she's at the top of the mountain. Not me. I'm not stupid. *You.* You're the one who believes it."

"You think my mother's still alive?" he said.

"I know she is and so do you."

"Why?"

"I already told you."

Suzy groaned and rolled her pinpoint eyes. When the doll was annoyed, sparks of temper popped behind plastic.

"Why wouldn't my dad tell me the truth?" Marshall asked.

Her eyes were looking directly at him, but also at everything, the way painted eyes can. Marshall lowered his head and studied the ground. Strange pulses surged through his chest. He looked at the rocks in his hands.

"Way back when you were still a human," he said. "You told me your parents said that they weren't giving up on you...but that they were giving up on an indifferent world."

The wind was whipping. Marshall began to shiver. He was wearing a thick, sturdy jacket, a long undershirt, and a polyester overshirt, but the cold still went straight through him.

"Get rid of those stupid rocks in your hands," she said.

"Why?"

"Throw the rocks or I'll throw them for you."

Marshall tossed the rocks into the woods and they disappeared silently into the snow. He stood there, looking to where they lay. The wind was blowing at his back. Snow coated his shoulders. Marshall tightened the strap on his hood, pulling it tightly around his forehead and chin.

The doll was becoming impatient, looking about,

eyes squinting as the wind touched them with a rush of brittle flakes. She ordered Marshall to start hiking and they trudged on in silence.

***

Every so often the sun would make its way through the clouds and the light would be diffused through the mist. A coyote yelped far away, a pair of high-pitched cries like an animal taken by surprise. A few seconds later there was another yelp, even farther away.

The snow blanketed trees, blanketing everything, whole drifts tumbling from branches. Marshall sniffed the air and caught the scent of decay. It was not human, but the kind of scent given off by oily, unwashed hair. Usually he could tell from which direction a scent emanated, but this scent was scattered through the wind.

He was thirsty, but they only had two bottles of water and one was almost finished. He was tempted to open his mouth and drink the snow, but his father would get mad if he knew. Eating snow lowered the body's core temperature. Instead, he bit into an apple, the sweetness claiming his mouth.

They came to a frozen lake and waterfall. The sun

was low and a stray ray illuminated the slithering flow behind the ice. The small lake, no larger than half an Olympic swimming pool, was covered in a thick layer of snow. Low groans of shifting ice broke through the stillness. In the alcove of the lake, near the waterfall, sounds were corralled.

Suzy stopped Marshall at the edge of the lake and waved her cupped hand in the air. She did not turn around, but hushed him, and pointed.

"A coyote," she whispered.

Within a stone's throw, a coyote was peering from behind a tree, its brown and white mane frosted by a light black fur. It stood unsteadily on its legs, back sagging, eyes yellow and crusted. Its coat was clumped and mulching. There were icicles on its mane and sores peeking from its hind legs, purple and maroon blushes against white skin. The animal knew they had spotted it, but instead of hiding, remained crouched. It was panting even though the temperature was close to freezing.

"She looks sick," Suzy said.

As the animal raised its head, its sunken black eyes focused upon them. Marshall held out his finger and approached. He raised his hands and waved them in the air. The animal tapped its front teeth together, then arched its back, uttering a low, gurgling sound.

Suzy motioned for Marshall to back up onto the ice, but the coyote slowly stepped forward, keeping its eyes upon them. They stepped farther out. Marshall knew that the coyote wouldn't follow them out onto the frozen lake. Animals were afraid of ice. Still, he kept backing up, farther than was necessary. When the coyote stopped on the lake's bank, where the rocks sloped into the water, Suzy sighed with relief; "She'll go now."

"I don't like this," he said.

"Me neither."

"This is our mountain too," Marshall said, glaring. "We're allowed to be here. I'm not afraid of this coyote. If it wants to fight us, let it fight us. If it loses, I'm going to kill it."

Suzy turned and eyed Marshall sternly, but he did not meet her eyes. Instead, he kept his gaze locked on the coyote.

"We're not going to fight it," Suzy said.

"It's not right," Marshall said.

"What's not right?"

"We are allowed to be here, just as much as she is. If she's sick, she should die."

"It's a coyote," the doll said.

"So."

"She doesn't understand right and wrong."

Suddenly, Marshall charged the coyote, screaming and waving his hands in the air. The animal hissed and retreated. Marshall laughed tauntingly, then spit at the animal. Suzy shouted, "*Stop!*" The coyote stepped forward again. Marshall jogged backward and the coyote followed, leaping several feet onto the ice before stopping. Marshall bounded forward, nearly ramming the animal. The coyote leapt backward, forelegs skating about, rear legs collapsing on the ice. It hesitated at the edge, not willing to be tricked twice. Marshall stopped as well, far out on the ice. They both stood their ground, eyes reading one another. He waved his hands and the coyote flinched, crouched, touching its chin to the snow.

Marshall took a step forward and so did the coyote. The ice cracked. Water percolated. He lost his footing, dropped to his knees. The ice opened, crack giving way to cracks. Marshall's foot slipped. He dropped Suzy, and she slid in with the rest of the snow, gliding between a narrow opening. He screamed, thrusting his hand in the lake, but the doll had sunk into the depths of the water.

The Panic was fully awake, stretching and yawning, flapping its wings and breathing fire. The Fury was growling, roiling about in his body.

The coyote rushed forward. Marshall screamed and swung his backpack. The coyote backed away and growled, fangs out. He threw the backpack at the coyote, leapt off the ice, dove into the lake. It wasn't deep, maybe ten feet, and Marshall swam quickly to the bottom. He caught his clothes on submerged branches. The water pricked, hot then freezing then hot again. The cold was unrelenting, pressing heavily against his chest. He clawed his way back to the surface, treading water and gasping.

He saw the coyote rooting around his backpack, picking at jerky and apples. Marshall dove back under the water and patted around the rocky bottom. He surfaced, went back under, resurfaced, each time becoming more furious that the coyote's snout was deeper in his backpack.

On the fourth attempt, Marshall found Suzy lodged between two rocks. He snatched her tiny body and raced to the surface. When his head was above the water, he clawed for a piece of solid ice, but it splintered in his hand. He grabbed a rock along the shore, but it was too slick. He attempted to pull himself onto an even thicker piece of ice, but it too broke. He was kicking with all his might, but his wet clothes pulled at his limbs. Water flooded into his mouth. Suzy was screaming vague commands.

The Panic roared. The Fury squealed. The Fury reached out and grabbed the coyote's forelegs and the animal was so surprised that, at first, it didn't even react.

When the animal realized what was happening, it snapped at Marshall's hand, piercing the flesh between his thumb and forefinger.

With several hard tugs, Marshall dragged the animal closer. The coyote dug her paws into the ice, but Marshall used his weight as a counterbalance. When the edge of the ice cracked, just under the coyote, Marshall knew he had won. He gave one last hard pull and the coyote lost its footing.

The coyote went under, then seconds later surfaced, thrashing about, huffing, spitting. There was a frantic whirl of teeth, claws, ice, arms, and hands. Marshall used the animal's franticness against itself, shoving the coyote under and climbing on its back. Each time the animal bit him, Marshall bit right back, flat teeth grinding into its bony neck. Realizing that the boy would not let go, the coyote swam toward shore, paddling through the frozen lake, breaking the ice with its paws.

They were silent in the snowy dusk, the only sound that of the coyote breaking through the ice as she swam. By the time they reached the waterfall, the animal was spent, tongue lolled onto ice-crusted rock, gasping in the shallows. Touching his feet to the bottom, Marshall pulled himself from the water, crawled along the edge of the waterfall, dragged himself to dry land, and collapsed into a snowdrift. The coyote followed, scraping its weary body along the rocks. In the dusty winter light, steam plumed from their bodies.

Marshall gazed at the animal. The Fury was still roiling. He rose from the snow, clothes and hair dripping, crouched over a half-submerged rock, pried it free. He lifted the large rock in both hands, wobbled over to the coyote, and lofted it above his head. The coyote was looking up at him with sulphur-colored eyes.

The rock was trembling in his hands, blackened water dripping onto the white ground.

"Be merciful," Suzy murmured, from in his pants pocket.

Marshall did not respond, but remained standing with the rock aloft. His mind was becoming confused again, like it had at the juvenile center. He felt dizzy and unsure.

"She did nothing wrong," Suzy said. "She was just trying to survive. Like you."

"I am not an animal."

Marshall was shivering. Tears swelled through the condensation on his face. He sat down next to the coyote, put the rock in his lap, touched his hand to the coyote's nose, and felt her breath upon his fingers. Moving his hand over the animal's eyes, he pulled the eyelids closed and when they opened again, he put his wet hat over her eyes so that she could not see what he was about to do.

***

Dusk cast a silver streak across the lake, sparking the snowflakes. The columns of powder-covered trees stood like a ghostly phalanx against the darkening sky. The cold infiltrated Marshall's skin, seeping into his muscles and bones.

He peeled off his clothes and underwear, and the cold air stung his wet, bare skin. Naked except for boots, he went around the lake's perimeter, crouched by his backpack, put on the spare clothes taken from the van. He unrolled his sleeping bag, wrapped it around his body, and hummed "Gangnam Style" as he spread out the contents of his bag. He ate a fruit bar in two bites, then peeled the wrapper and licked the sweet crumbs inside.

He gathered a small amount of wood, constructed a pyramid from the scrap, and flicked the lighter, but it was wet from being in the lake. It took nearly twenty minutes before the flame burned long enough to start a fire.

When the fire was going, he hung his clothes out to dry, circled the pit, and stomped his feet for circulation.

The cold and the fight with the coyote had drained his energy. The fruit bar and apple had only left him craving more food.

He went to the dead coyote, picked up her front paw, gave a hard tug, and dragged her body to the light of the fire. He opened a pocketknife he had also taken from the van. It was dull, the hinges flimsy, and when it snapped closed, it nearly sliced his hand. Holding the knife at an angle, he stabbed it into the coyote's rear, just under the tail, cutting its flank inch by inch, until he could pry his fingers under the flesh. He cut down to the coyote's rear legs and yanked out the guts, chopped pieces of the coyote's hindquarters into oblong cubes, and tossed them on the fire as the coals popped, snapped, dimmed.

He continued to skin the coyote, concentrating through his shivering. Still, he was surprised at how easily the skin came off, far easier than that of a squirrel or a deer.

He hung the coyote skin along with his wet clothes, hunched over the flesh, and began to carve chunks from the legs and back. He tossed them in and they sizzled against the coals, browning then blackening.

Using twigs as prongs, Marshall pulled the meat out of the flames and let the chunks cool in the snow. The skin was charred and the inside was red, but they tasted like the buffalo sandwiches he and his father ate at the county fair. Marshall couldn't chew fast enough, and, because the chunks were so gritty, it was hard to swallow. He didn't have the energy to cut more meat so he closed his eyes and slumped over. Suzy called out, but her voice was far away, as if she had been dropped down a drainpipe.

Marshall groaned and looked at the doll. Her peach plastic skin was lambent in the firelight. Her eyebrows dipped and she studied her hands as if lost in thought. She looked up at Marshall with worry, then slowly her expression became that of when he first found her, the Playmobil factory-standard smile, the round eyes hardening into dots.

"We're going to die if we go to the top of the mountain," Suzy said. "You have to listen to me."

He closed his eyes and tried to slip into sleep.

"Do you know what I am?" Suzy asked.

"You're Suzy DeGreer," he murmured.

Her frown was of a preacher about to loose predictions.

"I'll tell you," she said. "Listen carefully. *I am the last thing that keeps you from becoming what people think you are.*"

He grunted.

"Did you hear me?" she asked.

"I heard you."

"What did I say?"

He did not answer. She pulled his eyelids open. "I said, *I am the last thing that keeps you from becoming what people think you are.*"

***

A permanent chill spread and hardened. Currents of energy, hot and sharp, drifted down his spine. He knew that if he did not get to sleep soon, then tomorrow he could not make it to the top of the mountain.

He constructed a small shelter about ten feet from the fire, building it with pine branches and packing the in-between nooks with needles. He finished quickly, packing the walls with snow and dirt. When he sat down inside the shelter, he was struck by the silence. There was not a single hole or draft to let the air whistle through, not a creak or groan from the wood when the storm pressed against it.

He warmed his hands by the fire, blew on the fire's coals, threw on more wood. The pieces burned rapidly, sticks crackling into orange tubes. The snowflakes sizzled as they hit the flames.

As the moon rose, the coyotes called to one another, their howls winding through the dark mass of pines. He got up and dragged the dead coyote back out to the lake and dropped her onto the ice. It was a warning. The scent of the carcass would blow across the frozen expanse of the lake and into the adjacent forest.

He stumbled back, but was overcome with cramps. He buckled to his knees, squinting through the pain. Across the lake, serpents of flakes rose then tumbled, clumps of snow falling from the pine branches and making a loud *whump*. On the other side of the forest, he glimpsed the shadows of dozens of coyotes, leaning together in a half-circle, just like the boys from the juvenile center.

***

The moon was in descent. The snowflakes flittered downward, fibers twirling midair. The clouds were a filament. The temperature had dropped below zero.

He looked over his arms and hands. The coyote had mauled his right hand, puncturing the skin in a dozen places. The blood had dried so that his knuckles and fingers resembled a lumpy, gnarled claw.

The coyote's intestines were lying near the shelter. He lay on his side and gnawed at the ends. The rubber saltiness was as refreshing as manna.

***

He was sleeping, but he woke long enough to feel Elway licking the back of his thigh, his hand. Marshall rose from the feverish depths of dreams, surfacing like a child in surf. It was a dream, but it was not a dream because chills were engulfing him. He could not stop shaking. He squeezed Elway close, told him he loved him two, three times, although he wasn't sure his lips were moving. He smelled the dog one more time and fell into a deep sleep.

X

Jace had slept poorly—Leslie's grated breathing, worries about Marshall. His ribs ached deep from within the bone. As he sat up, his phone vibrated. He pulled it out. He had received a message from Ozzie.

"ETA 9:30 A.M. 12+"

The *12+* meant that the mountain's entire search and rescue were heading his way, twelve men and women hiking out with sleds before dawn.

Jace pushed himself up with his elbows, his head clear, eyes dry, eyelids chapped. As he tried to stand, his head spun into blackness. He dug out two more ibuprofen, buried at the bottom of his backpack, and swallowed them dry.

He packed quickly then attended to Leslie one last time, checking patches, heart rate, pupils. The attendant's pulse had slowed to a healthier rate. A good sign. He had stabilized.

He gathered as much wood as he could, built a fire a good distance from the cave so that search and rescue could easily spot the smoke. He warmed himself up, filled his canteen with snow, and boiled it on the coals and, as he waited, scanned the mountain with his binoculars.

His start was slow. His lungs hurt more than the day before, pincers in his guts. He hacked blood constantly as he followed a single, narrow footpath, a winding route that slipped between boulders and clumps of pine. There were coyote tracks, a few signs of deer. The smaller birds glided upon the crusty surface.

He stopped frequently, surveying the mountain. The cloud breaks were at the lower elevations, opening into vaporous gaps. At this high altitude, he had to breathe harder and when he paused, he gripped the throbbing in his ribs. Deep in the forest, where the snow could not entirely penetrate the trees, Marshall's prints were still visible. They were clear tracks that veered here and there, but left no doubt to their direction.

Above the tree line, the peaks reappeared, vast and encompassing. This was his favorite part of the mountain, where, on a good day, he could see well over a hundred miles down the valley. How many times had he hiked and camped up here, just above the tree line, watching the sun rise and later set against those peaks? How many times, after Marshall was asleep, had he and Lynne talked then made love next to the campfire while the peaks loomed in the darkness? The memories and the familiarity of the terrain gave him strength.

***

Jace tracked Marshall's prints to a lake as wide as the granite peaks were tall. Trees surrounded the lake on either side, but standing in front of the water, they gave the impression of a skating rink walled by pines. In the summer, the daylong hike brought campers to swim and was often frequented by the kind of healthy teenagers who preferred rock climbing to off-roading, silence over loud music. The water was clear but cold, fed by a spring emerging from under a towering boulder. The spring mysteriously built upon itself, swelling into a waterfall on the north end, which this time of year was frozen into a collection of icicles as thick as organ pipes.

Jace filled his canteen with water and dropped in a purification tablet. As he stood there, swishing the water to dissolve the tablet, he noticed that the ice was broken in several places. There were no tracks, but the cracks extended the length of the lake. There were no footprints, no indication that someone had been walking upon the ice. Instead, it looked like someone or something had recently swum across.

On the far north side of the lake, Jace glimpsed a structure, like a fallen stork's nest. Following the edge of the shore, his boots crunching through the thin edges of ice, it took him fifteen minutes to reach the makeshift shelter. He swallowed his excitement as he ran his hand over the shelter as if divining its origin. The branches had been crossed and stitched together. The needles were mixed with snow to keep out the wind.

A tornado of snow made its way across the lake and when it struck the shelter, it became crazed under its own maleficence. The hut, which looked as if it could buckle from the blast, barely quivered. Jace looked out over the lake then back at the shelter.

There were tracks, three-pronged prints, too big to be a coyote. One set of tracks went to the edge of the lake and stopped at an avocado-shaped mound. Jace had overlooked it at first because it was coated in a light sheet of snow. He saw it was a dead coyote, encapsulated in an icy crust. He knelt down and touched the frozen carcass and saw that the coyote had been skinned, the back of its skull crushed, the muscles along the hind legs hacked away, the intestines ripped out. The best cuts of meat had been removed. Jace choked with the recognition that this was Marshall's work. The boy had carved up the coyote exactly how Jace had taught him.

***

For the next hour, he passed orange signs with large black crosses: skiers beware. The tops of saplings no taller than his waist poked out from the snow. Any tree or bush that was not flexible had been flattened or carried down by the avalanches. There was nothing here. All was covered. The monochrome was dizzying. The clouds became indistinguishable from the fresh snow.

He stepped as quietly as possible, listening carefully for sounds that might be a warning. When he was almost out of avalanche alley, he heard a splitting of rock and the warbling echo of a mountain's mass in movement. He glimpsed a faint cloud of snow near the top of the mountain, smudging the edges of the sky with an alabaster sheen.

Jace gazed upward, shielding his eyes, and made out a narrow shuffling of white jigsaw pieces, a choppy cloud accumulating rapidly. The sound was like stones tumbling into a quarry. He knew exactly what it was. His body reacted instinctively—his eyes blurred, his muscles tightened, sweat built upon his back.

A hundred feet away a large rock was jutting out of the snow. It was angling out from the mountain, providing a small natural shelter. He gazed up the mountain. Everything was the same dusty white and it was nearly impossible to measure the movement of the rolling cloud.

You've climbed in these kinds of conditions thousands of times, he told himself. *You've been closer to more avalanches than this one. Take it easy. It's not coming your way.*

But every time he looked up, the plume was fanning farther outward, swelling in his direction, traveling two hundred miles an hour, hurling millions of pounds of matter in its wake.

A shadow descended. The ground around him was shifting. He started to run in the direction of the avalanche, toward the large boulder. He couldn't breathe. His head swooned. Each time he lifted a foot, his boots barely cleared the snow. He was crawling on his hands and knees the last few feet, spitting blood. He reached the rock just as the rumbling overtook the silence. The wind fleeing the fast-moving snow rushed past and the first spray touched his face.

Jace leaned as hard as he could against the boulder, holding his arms out in front of himself. The avalanche blew over, a crackling, spattering boom, the earth trembling, then filling in all around him. It went on for what seemed like hours, piling snow thicker and thicker, filling every corner and crevice.

***

Judging from the light in his snowy bubble, which had been quartered then halved, the tail end of the avalanche sprinkled its final dusting. As the till settled, rocks and pebbles drizzled through the fissures. There was a dull, uneven groan as tons of snow compressed under their own weight.

Panic churned in his gut then coated his body like a toxin. He took a deep breath, pursed his lips, and tensed his muscles. The adrenalin was draining.

The average time someone could live under an avalanche, with the lack of oxygen, was two minutes.

He pressed his hands against the ice and was stunned by its solidness. He punched it with his fist and shook off the sting. When he kicked it with his foot, shards flew in all directions, but he'd hardly made a dent. He exhaled, the moisture from his lungs crackling against the snow.

He closed his eyes, but not a single thought came. His mind was completely blank. Because there were no thoughts, no plan could be formed. Rubbing his palm into his eye, he let out a groan and shook off the fuzz swarming in his head. He coughed hard, a dry cough that had an iron aftertaste.

Blue cavities extended like veins into the body of the avalanche. He exhaled and a translucent cloud appeared as fast as it vanished. He knew there were only a few precious minutes left. Somewhere, though, in the back of his head, he had already given up. He had never heard of someone digging themselves out of an avalanche.

Sleep began to suck at his body, urging him toward the lull of unconsciousness. He forced himself awake, swimming out of a soupy darkness. Each inhalation felt colder and harsher, diluted by his own output of carbon dioxide. He dug into his backpack, took out a pocketknife, and began to chisel at the ice. Tiny little pieces came off like grains of sand. He dropped the knife.

***

Jace dozed off and was brought back to a time when he was a boy, no older than twelve years. He and his father were climbing near the top of the mountain, along Saw-tooth Ridge. As they ascended, Jace kept his eyes on his father's neck, thickened by military service, forearms shaped into pears from installing heavy asbestos roof tiles, thighs thickened into stumps from standing endless days on ladders.

They were heading toward a pond on the far west side of the mountain, a place where the water was so clear that the colored speckles of the rainbow trout reflected, even below the surface. Jace was carrying his backpack and their fishing gear. His father was whistling Schumann. Their German shepherd, Marino, named after the legendary Miami Dolphins quarterback, was not far behind.

Halfway up the mountain, it began to rain. Jace and his father put on their ponchos, surveyed the clouds, then continued on, leaning into the pine trees. They went up one switchback after another, the trail doubling upon itself as it cut into the mountainside.

As they rounded a corner, facing the dark belly of the storm, a blast flashed in front of them. Both Jace and his father were thrown to the ground. The boom that followed seconds later made their ears ring. A blast of bark came next, millions of shivers hurtling toward them. His father covered his head, but Jace looked up. Splinters slashed his face. Jace blacked out, and when he opened his eyes again, he glimpsed his frantic father shouting as the rain poured from his hair and cheeks. He fell back into unconsciousness and as the darkness took over heard his father calling his name, felt the man's rough hands stroking his cheeks.

Moving in and out of consciousness, Jace knew that his father was carrying him down the mountain. He had hoisted his son over his shoulder and was marching steadily through the rain. He did not stop or even pause for rest. He groaned on the heavier downward steps and occasionally murmured, "*Lord, please do not take my only son.*"

***

Jace awoke. His head was spinning. A crow was cawing above, the bird's call muffled through the snow. There was a groaning, the shifting and settling of the avalanche up the slope, thousands of tons of loose ice creating an uneasy foundation.

He rested his head on his knees and tried to breathe as lightly as possible. His lungs sounded like a handsaw pulled across soft timber.

He began digging again at the ice with his knife, but it was so compacted that each scrape barely made a groove. He could not breathe. His lungs burned. When he coughed, it felt as if it would never end.

***

He was taking shorter, faster breaths. His heart rate was increasing. The steam from his breath was no longer thick, but thin, like mushroom spores released into a draft. Each new inhalation left him gasping, parched. He took out his canteen and drank, but even drinking required undue exertion.

"Jace?" he heard a voice say. It was little more than a whisper.

Through the blue ice, several feet away, he made out a dark shape. There was something comforting about the vague outline like a lone, flickering candle in a darkened hallway.

"Jace," he heard again. He looked around for her voice, which seemed to be coming from everywhere, even right inside his cocoon. He tapped on the ice and the shadow's silhouette shifted ever so slightly.

"Lynne," he said.

The shadow shifted and for the first time he realized that indeed it was more, a being, a person, trapped here with him. He picked at the ice with his fingers. The shadow moved and he saw something in the shape of a hand touch the ice. It was a small hand, Lynne's hand. He could make out the outline of her fingers, something smooth and oblong, perhaps her wedding ring.

"It's not your fault," Lynne whispered. Her voice sounded as it did when they first met, camping high up on the mountain, smoking and drinking and making love under the stars.

"I love him," she said. "I do."

"I tried to do the right thing."

"There is no right thing."

"I had to give him hope. That's why he came here. To find you."

The silence connected them, became a conduit through the ice. He was sure he could hear her breathing.

The oxygen in his cave was almost gone. His lungs inhaled, but only filled with his own breath.

"Come back," he said.

She did not answer and for a second he suspected that she might have fled again. He pulled off his gloves and used what nails he had, scratching and clawing at the ice. Soon, he was digging with both hands, ice accumulating under his nails. He was digging so hard that his fingers began to bleed, coloring violet grooves into the azure ice.

The shadow did not move. She would wait for him, for as long as it took to tunnel through. He knew this. She would accept him all over again for who he was…for his stubbornness, for his blind determination.

The ice gave way, huge chunks crashing onto his lap. A current of fresh air flooded his tiny bubble. He gasped and spit. His consciousness sharpened into focus. Lynne was not there. There was nothing.

He was crying now. Blood covered his fingers. His nails were torn and partially peeled. He pressed his face to the hole. It smelled of pine and mud and wet rock.

***

Jace put on his gloves and punched at the hole until he could no longer feel his hand. Just beyond the hole was a crevasse. Sharp chunks of ice scraped his chest and belly. He wiggled inch by inch, clawing at the snow. With each exertion, the pain from his ribs intensified, and the strain became unbearable.

Pulling himself upward, he tugged his backpack behind him, and soon he was free. He came out onto a barren field of rocks, timber, and massive chunks of ice.

He pulled himself up and out and lay there, staring up at the thick clouds, panting, the falling snow brushing his face. He thought of nothing but Lynne, still energized by the wonder of her presence. And he continued to cry, not only with relief, but renewal.

XI

When Marshall awoke next to Elway, the dog fortified not only his strength, but his will. He got the fire going again, cooked some more meat, melted snow and poured it into his canteen. He gave Elway a fleshy coyote bone, but the dog turned his nose up at it.

"We're going to see my mom today," Marshall told Elway.

"He doesn't know what you are saying," Suzy said.

"He knows just as much as you do."

They set off as dawn was giving way to light filtered through clouds. Marshall was dizzy and walking was difficult. It took them a few hours to cover what should have only taken one.

Just before the tree line, the trail passed a collapsed shed. There were many abandoned mines on the mountain, but the shed had been used only as a shelter. The roof had caved in and the walls were sagging, but inside there were unopened cans of food, polyurethane barrels and jugs, stacks of magazines, and an old mattress resting upon milk crates.

Marshall stopped and surveyed the site. Suzy squirmed out from his pocket. The smells emanating from the shed were much like the coyotes, unwashed and earthen. He tested the shed's floorboards. They bowed and creaked under his weight. Through the slats he saw bare ground and frost shining like brushed lead.

The inside of the shed was about as tall as he was, designed for sitting or sleeping, but not for standing. It was about half the size of his bedroom. The boards on the walls were warped and gaps of light peaked through. Whoever had built the rickety structure had done a poor job. But aesthetics were not the point. The shelter was designed for someone's own, strange specificities; a chair facing a corner, a table covered in childlike stick figures, light bulbs lying on every surface, plastic toy dogs, of all shapes and sizes, piled atop a cracked bathroom tile. Marshall walked slowly through the shed and as he did, he felt a strange sense of comfort.

"It's quiet here," Marshall said.

"Too quiet."

"If we didn't have to go to the top of the mountain, we could stay here."

"Speak for yourself," Suzy said.

Marshall picked up a can of mandarin oranges lying on the floor and shook it next to his ear. He took out his pocketknife and started to pry open the top. As he worked the metal, juice spilled onto the ground, and Elway rushed over to lick it up. When Marshall finally got the can open, he drank the sweet fruit like juice, barely stopping to chew.

A hundred feet away, there was a pear-shaped boulder. Behind it was a large pine, which, years ago, had been split down the middle by a lightning strike. The trunk was growing into two separate trees that drooped away from each other, and a green and black moldy rope lay at its base.

Marshall set the fruit down and untied the rope. When it was loose, the trees bowed toward the ground. He wrapped the rope around the split tree once again. Then he looped it around his own body. He did this three times then pulled as hard as he could, tugging the rope until it was tight around his body. Blood rushed to his face and head, the timber pressed against his shirt, splinter shards and bark poked his skin. He pulled again until he could not breathe.

Gradually, the trees melted. The forest was breathing, blowing the scent of pine and sap. The pressure was enough for him to hear his mother, her voice a faint wisp floating upon the wind, in the ground, in the pine trees and in the clouds. He let go of the rope, it slackened, and Marshall slumped over. He listened to the air entering and leaving his lungs. The mountain was misted in clouds. A fresh bank of clouds was approaching, stretching from the earth to the cloudy sky like a sail extended.

"You know who I think lives here?" Marshall said.

"I think I know who *you* think lives here."

"Kid Colter," he said quickly. When Suzy didn't respond, he added, "What if Kid Colter is like me?"

"I would tell him he should try and adapt to the world, instead of running away from it."

"What if he couldn't?" Marshall said. "What if it was impossible for him to fit in? Kid Colter was invisible. I want to be invisible. Then I could just be me. No one would care how I behaved. Everyone would stop trying to make me be someone different."

Suzy rolled her eyes. "Being alone is easy, but it's not healthy."

The trembling in his muscles was returning. His stomach was still queasy and the canned food sat stiff in his belly.

The sharp edge of a mirror was poking out from under a stack of magazines, a shard from a much larger mirror. He had never liked mirrors. They always left him unsettled, as if he were looking at someone pretending to be him. But now he was jolted by what he saw. His face was bloodless, his eyes bruised, his hair oily. He looked like some of the badly wounded people he and his dad found on search and rescue.

"Let's go," Marshall said. "My mom is waiting for us."

***

They left the shed and followed a low, protected ridge. By early afternoon, they were traversing a narrow trail that threaded the mountain's spine and exposed them to the brunt of the wind. The gusts were uncompromising, the kind of wind that moved without restraint, gales so severe that the snow never landed, but recirculated through the clouds.

The wind was whipping across the landscape. The top layer became an unsteady mass. The powder steamed from the peaks and into the sky. The cold slipped through Marshall's jacket, squirming through the fabric and clinging to his skin. He was wearing the coyote hide around his neck and the tail flapped against his back, chittering like a flag in a hurricane.

Again and again, Marshall stumbled, landing face

forward into a drift. When he reached the last part of the ascent, he stepped cautiously along a cornice, but was not even halfway before the snow gave. He slid a dozen feet, but stopped by digging in with his feet and clenching the icy wall with his numb fingers. He clambered back, was met by Elway's wet tongue, and continued to crawl the last few hundred feet up the mountain, hand in front of hand, knee in front of knee.

When they were near the top, the clouds thinned as the storm regrouped. The sun broke through the clouds and scattered translucent beams along the slopes. Marshall managed to stand and stumble over to an arête, holding the granite outcropping tightly. He took off his gloves. The tips of his fingers were deep purple while other parts were yellowy and transparent. Frostbite was setting in. Still, he told himself not to worry. He had seen amputations from frostbite on YouTube. Finger, toes, noses, lips. The body could be taken away, piece by piece, and still function.

The last few steps were easier. He pawed his way forward. At the top, the mountain was flat. The wind was at his back, thrusting him forward. He lay down and closed his eyes. He could still hear the wind, which was battering his neck and face, but he could no longer see the storm. There was a repetitive symphony of wind and hard snow drumming against his hat and jacket.

Marshall had expected to find his mother waiting for him and even imagined falling into her arms while she took him to someplace safe. However, she was not here and he could not bear to hear Suzy say I told you so.

Suzy was screaming into the wind, though her words did not sound urgent, but more conciliatory, as if she were reassuring him after one of his tantrums.

As Marshall lay there, he felt his leg muscles stiffen, his feet cramp, and his muscles go numb.

"A house," Suzy said.

"She'll come."

"A house," Suzy repeated. "We'll even make a room for your mother. Just like we did with your Duplo house."

He lifted Suzy up and looked into her eyes. The doll's face was stoic.

"She'll come?" he asked.

Suzy did not answer. Marshall pushed himself to his feet. He looked around, found the biggest snowdrift, and crawled on his knees, digging and tunneling into the hardened snow. He kept his head down, clawing out chunks, firing an icy spray from between his legs. He sang gently,

Oppa Gangnam style
Gangnam style

Op, op, op, op
Oppa Gangnam style
Gangnam style

He tunneled out the entryway and dug out a bedroom, shoveling the snow outward, between his legs. When he finished, he crawled back outside, patted the shell of the cave until it was smooth and clean. He tried writing his name in big, block letters, just above the top, but could only really write MARSHA because the double *L*s confused him.

His vision was becoming fuzzy and he wasn't sure if he was dizzy or the snow was blinding him. His body trembled, his blood felt as if it were freezing. He forced himself to sit against a rock and closed his eyes, listening to the wind.

"You *have* to get inside," Suzy said.

Marshall closed his eyes again. He was slipping away, into blackness. A warm wetness trickled down his face. He recognized, as his therapist had taught him, that his tears were from disappointment. "Disappointment," he had learned, was the process of wanting something, but not getting it. With toys or games, "disappointment" was a straightforward feeling while being "disappointed" in people was complex, involving memories, relationships, someone's past and present behavior.

Another sensation, dull and leaden, washed over him. This emotion involved retracing events, ordering them into a conclusion, and then making an assessment. It required prediction, judgment, and critique. This emotion, he had been taught in therapy, was called "doubt."

***

He was too weak to pull himself inside the snow hut, so he called out for the dog. Elway did not come. He tried to call for the dog again, but his mouth was stuck, his tongue swollen, and his throat was closing up on itself.

The doll took his hand, whispered something that he could not hear, but which he knew was encouraging, and together they crawled inside. Marshall paused before plugging the doorway with snow. A heavy silence descended. Finding Elway on the mountain had given him hope. Now, without the dog, without his mother, without his father, he felt as if he'd been abandoned by everyone except Suzy.

He struggled to take his sleeping bag out of his backpack, unroll it, and lay it next to the doll. His clothes were damp, but he was too cold to move or stretch out.

"When do you think my mom will come?" he asked Suzy.

"I can't answer that," she said.

"And my dad?"

"I don't know."

"You don't know…"

He pulled his jacket closed, yanked down his hat, and curled into a ball. He remembered that his father had taught him that you must mark snow caves, so he considered crawling toward the entrance. But his body could give no more.

"Close your eyes," Suzy said.

"They won't find us. If I don't mark the cave."

"Think of food," Suzy said. "Good food."

"Chocolate?"

"Anything warm and with sugar."

"Pancakes."

The floor was spinning. He felt sick to his stomach. Turning on his side, he vomited.

"Pancakes," Suzy said.

Marshall closed his eyes as tightly as he could and thought of a fresh stack of pancakes. There were at least ten, piled a foot high. They were all for Marshall. They were his alone to eat. They were steaming, the butter and maple syrup slipping down the side. There was a container of powdered sugar that he could sprinkle on top. A jar of his mother's strawberry jam.

XII

The avalanche had left a trail of destruction, a jumbled till of rocks, trees, and branches. The forest at the lower elevation had been wiped clean, timbers stripped and blasted south, pointing like accusing fingers.

The snowfall had picked up and the wind blew stiff against his face. Pain spread like thistles under his skin, just above the bone of his sternum.

He had melted water before leaving, but even as the sun reached a quarter of its rise, most of it was gone. Every time the tracks disappeared, he began to worry. When they reappeared, he choked with elation.

When the last of the trees gave way to rock and ice, Jace took a break, dropping heavily against a drift. He glimpsed a figure sprinting through the forest. At first he thought it was a deer or a coyote. There hadn't been wolves on the mountain for years. The animal was headed straight toward him, traveling swiftly. The size, color, and speed were like nothing he had ever seen.

He reached for his backpack, rifling the contents for a weapon. The animal was bolting through the snow, a beige flash, disappearing and reappearing like a ray of light. Slowly, he recognized Elway, his tongue lolling in dopey, urgent bliss.

The dog barreled into him. Elway licked him frenetically while Jace struggled to push him off.

The dog climbed on him, pressing against his sore ribs. When Jace pushed him off, Elway gazed at him with impatience, tail thumping the snow flat.

While Jace was catching his breath, pressing his hand against his ribs, Elway loped back up the mountain, stopping after a hundred feet. The Labrador's light-colored coat blended with the snow and the rocks and the trees. His tail swept the air, his body taut and arched. He came running back and stared at Jace questioningly, then sprinted off again, waiting at a distance.

Jace had hated the idea of paying money for a purebred when there were so many dogs at the shelter. Lynne, however, argued that Labradors were good for kids, especially for one as combustible as Marsh. Jace gave in, drove to a kennel on the other side of the mountain, and paid hundreds for the yellow Lab pup.

Lynne had been right. Elway understood Marsh. The dog fled before the Panic and the Fury started, and showed up, affectionate and forgiving, when it was all over. No matter how often Jace cleaned the sheets, the end of Marshall's bed was always speckled with golden hair.

***

Down below, the valley was lost to the clouds. The wind and snow came so hard that Jace pulled his hood down and he was forced to shield his eyes with his gloves. He had hiked up this ridge maybe a dozen times, mostly in the summer, and had forgotten how narrow it was, how the drop on either side was misleading, falling into something not as sheer as a cliff, but nonetheless an unscalable descent.

When he came to an outcropping of granite, insulated from the wind, he gazed into the storm. At this elevation, the storm was little more than a tumultuous conflagration, dense precipitation morphing into a solid screen. Exasperated by Jace's slow pace, the dog ran back and forth, reaching some imaginary boundary then bounding back.

Jace started and fell and tried pushing himself to his feet. His elbows buckled. He coughed and spots of red blood landed in the snow. He closed his eyes and listened to the air churning. The snow did not land, but moved like a swarm. The dog was breathing in his ear, nudging him. Jace pushed the animal away. Elway nudged him again.

He got back up, followed the dog along the spine of the peak. Elway stopped and began circling in front of a drift, pressing his snout into a mound of snow. He never would have stopped here if it hadn't been for the dog. Indeed, there was something strange about the mound, an abnormality at this elevation. Jace brushed away the top powder and recognized that the snow had been compressed by hand.

He felt around the side of the mound until he found the thinnest layer. Slowly, he pushed. The snow gave. A small entrance appeared. Elway popped into the cave, sniffing along the entranceway. Jace broke a bigger hole, climbed through, then trailed the dog, crawling along a short tunnel which led to a small alcove. Almost immediately, he recognized a human shape in a fetal position.

Relief thrummed through his muscles and his whole body seized with joy. He grabbed Marshall and held him tightly. The boy moaned as Jace ran his hands over the boy's form, kissed his forehead again and again.

He kissed his son's ear. Kissed his son's forehead. Kissed his son's neck. He put his cheek to Marshall's cheek. There were swaths of frostbite on Marshall's face and hands. Bite marks, scratches, and cuts covered his arms and neck. Dozens of wounds had purpled or become infected. Most of Marshall's skin was blushed, not translucent, meaning the frostbite hadn't completely taken root.

Throwing his gloves off, Jace checked Marshall's pulse. It was fast, too fast; a fever, infection, hypothermia. He took off his own jacket and felt the sting of cold through his sweaty fleece. He rubbed his hands along the boy, creating a brief kick of warmth, then wrapped his jacket around him.

Using his knife, he cut his backpack's stitching and snapped apart the inside frame. He removed medical tape and, crouching as he followed the doorway, went back outside. The storm clasped earth and sky in its gray maw. Jace strapped the broken backpack pieces together, refitting them into an eight-foot pole. He cut a piece from his backpack and tied it to the pole. He plunged the flag into the highest point of the drift, then jerked it back and forth.

He leaned against the outside of the hut, panting. The snow was circulating, rising from far below, sliding upward along the dark slopes, neither landing nor falling. Snow plumes twirled upon his pants and coat. The wind was deafening. The coldness burned his eyes. There was no sense, no reason. Protons, neutrons, molecules, bashing and bumbling, tearing down, piling up, freezing, cracking, remolding. There was no meaning, but there was an undeniable harmony.

***

In the bitter light from his LED lamp, Jace made out his son's frosty exhalation migrating into the air. He touched his hand to Marshall's cheek. When Marshall coughed, Jace pulled him close. The boy opened one eye and smiled faintly. Jace felt his stomach lurch. All this time hiking up the mountain, he had been driven by the mechanics of purpose. Now that he had found Marshall, his emotions were congealing into relief.

He kissed Marshall's cheek, ran his hands through his hair. Marshall was hot, his body temperature far higher than it should be in this cold cave.

"Mom?" Marshall asked.

When Jace could not produce an answer, Marshall seemed resigned to the truth. He asked, "Elway?"

"He's here," Jace said and kissed Marshall's forehead. The boy's skin was hot.

Marshall closed his eyes, drifting off. Jace grabbed his son's face with two hands, pressed his nose against Marshall's temple, and felt his warm breath against the boy's skin. "You made it up in this storm."

"Why?" Marshall asked.

"I need you. No matter what we're dealt. I need you."

"Why?"

"Please don't say 'why' right now. Say anything else."

After a few seconds, Marshall murmured, "*Geurae neo hey, geurae baro neo hey.*"

Jace brought his ear closer to Marshall's mouth.

"*Jigeumbuteo gal dekkaji gabolkka.*"

It took Jace a second to understand what Marshall was saying, but once he did, they reprised softly together, as they had done so many times before, together, at home in bed, or camping:

> *Oppa Gangnam style*
> *Gangnam style*
> *Op, op, op, op*
> *Oppa Gangnam style*
> *Gangnam style*

XIII

As night approached and the temperature dropped, the storm gathered force. In their winter womb, Jace could hear only the muffled roar of the gales. The wind was in constant flux, its ferocity negated by its own regularity. Elway was curled nearby, his ear twitching every so often.

Jace removed his own clothes except for his long underwear, wrapped his son and himself in a sleeping bag, and covered them in a thin emergency tarp that he had brought from the van. Almost immediately, Jace could feel the warmth from his own body seeping away, transferring to Marshall.

***

Jace's own coughing woke him time and again. His

thoughts slipped off without reaching a conclusion. His mind drifted away without any warning.

Suzy had fallen from Marshall's hand and onto the snowy floor. She lay there, looking up at Jace almost pleadingly. It was morbid, he thought, this doll, but it had helped his son internalize the loss of his best friend.

Suzy DeGreer had been an autistic girl that Marshall sometimes played with. Her mother, Delilah, had set up the appointments every month or so, and the two children played contentedly, backs to one another. Last year, Suzy's father, a man who worked three jobs to cover their costs, left a note saying that he was leaving the family. The next day, Delilah, having no friends or relatives, and only a job as a gas station cashier, packed Suzy up in the car, went on a picnic, and then drove them both into a lake.

Jace and Marshall heard about Suzy's death on the local news. The boy had been silent for some time. Eventually, he asked, almost curiously, "Suzy, mountain with Mom now?"

***

Jace ran his hands along Marshall's body, looking for any missed scrapes or cuts. How many times had he washed

Marshall in the bathtub or the shower? How many times had he clothed him, cleaned him, cut his nails, stitched, bandaged, rubbed sunscreen on his appendages, practiced various sense therapies, and held the boy to the ground when he was having a violent breakdown?

Jace no longer felt the soft arms and legs of a boy. Soon, Marshall would have facial and body hair, muscles equal to his own. How could he restrain Marshall's Fury and Panic in twenty or thirty years, when he was in his prime and Jace was physically in decline?

The future was so long and so very unsure. Visions of Marshall homeless, locked up in prison, medicated into submission in an institution ran through his mind. He was too weak to push them away.

Maybe Marshall could survive when I die, Jace thought.

The boy had climbed to the top of the mountain, in a terrible winter storm, but Jace knew that surviving on the mountain and surviving in the social care system were entirely different things.

Or maybe Lynne was right, he considered, as he drifted off into sleep. *Maybe she was right all along.*

***

In his dream, he and Lynne were at a barbecue with friends. The mountain loomed in the distance, reflecting the sunset. As usual, the conversation turned to Marshall, questions posed as if their only child were a problem who needed solving by collective wisdom.

They had learned to hold hands through these advice-giving sessions, leaning into each other protectively as their friends dispensed well-intentioned, useless advice. Saying, "*Make sure you set boundaries. Children need boundaries,*" was, to Jace and Lynne, similar to a lifeguard shouting to a drowning man, "*Make sure you swim.*"

As Lynne and Jace rode home, they laughed about the inanity of their friends' comments.

"Matt told me we should use a sticker reward chart," Jace said, "until he outgrows his autism."

When they got home, the babysitter, Janine, a girl who'd grown up with a severely handicapped sister, met them at the door with a smile. She said that Marsh had been well-behaved all night, with only one tantrum over washing his hands. They had played hide-and-seek, and then watched a movie. For Jace and Lynne, it was equally bizarre as it was encouraging to hear a babysitter say that she had enjoyed herself.

Lynne and Jace stood in the kitchen, holding one another, watching Marshall walk in circles, rocking his head and chatting with Suzy. Lynne took the boy by the hand and told him it was time to go to bed. Jace lay back and opened a beer. As Lynne shadowed Marshall, trying to get him in his pajamas and brush his teeth, Jace watched sports highlights. At some point, he heard Lynne shouting, her patience cracking. She was trying to brush Marshall's teeth, but the boy was lying on the ground.

Jace turned to see Marshall attempting to flee and Lynne blocking his escape. His young muscles were as strong as they were limber, but Lynne had the determination of a mother cornered. When Marshall attempted to climb through her legs, she clasped him with her knees. Lynne reached out and grabbed him by the wrist. That was when Jace heard the boy's teeth come down upon her fingers, an unholy crunch on bone. Jace leapt from his chair and sprinted down the hallway.

Screeching, Marshall kicked the shower door. He kicked it again and again and as Jace rushed to stop him, the glass cracked and caved. Shards fell upon Marshall, slicing his shirt and back, but the boy was still kicking the door, as if unaware that more glass was falling.

He pulled Marshall out of the shower, but the boy was squirming and struggling to get free, not even hearing Jace's soothing words. He was slick with blood and slipped from Jace's grasp, sprinted out the back door, across the street, and toward the woods.

While Lynne was at the hospital getting her bitten finger stitched, Jace circled the neighborhood in his truck. Twice, he ran a stop sign. Once, he swerved, almost hitting a rabbit. Eventually, Marshall appeared in the road, walking toward the truck, crying, hitting himself in the head. The boy was covered in mud and branches, fists clenched in anger while his body trembled from sobbing. His shirt was soaked in blood. Jace stopped the truck, leapt out, grabbed the boy, held him and kissed him until he whimpered to be let go. As Jace struggled to tow Marshall off the road and back to the truck, the sheriff pulled up, clambered out of his Crown Vic, and shined his flashlight on the father and son.

"You two alright?"

The question was as absurd as his predicament. No one was alright. Everyone was suffering in their own way.

"You need anything?" the sheriff asked, his expression that of dry anticipation.

There was no answer to this question. The question itself suggested that a man holding his son in the middle of the road, in the middle of the night, while the mother was in the hospital for an injury made by her son, was "normal."

Jace's phone rang.

"Did you find him?" Lynne asked, on the other end.

"What about you?" Jace asked.

"Tell me you found him."

"I found him."

Lynne gasped and covered the phone and wept between hyperventilations. "My sweet boy," she said through tears.

"He's okay."

"He's okay."

"I'm bringing him to the hospital," he said.

"He bit through my cartilage, Jace. Right through. I can't imagine what the doctor's thinking."

"Who cares what the doctor thinks."

"I have to go to surgery. This needs surgery." She paused, as if listening to instructions from a distance. "I want to see him. I want to hold him. But, you know what? And don't let him hear this. I have to tell you. I'm disgusted with him, Jace. I'm disgusted with our son and, at the same time, I hate myself for being disgusted. I love him more than anything. And sometimes…sometimes I just hate him. I hate him so, so much."

"It's going to be okay."

"It's not going to be okay," she said. "It hasn't been okay for a long time. You know it. I know it. Oh. I love you. I do. I love Marshall, too. So much. Can I talk to him? I need to hear his voice."

Jace put the phone to Marshall's ear. The boy listened and occasionally pulled back, looking at the phone as if his mother were inside. Marshall had never liked phones, and even now, with his mother gushing words of love, he was silent.

He pushed the phone closer to Marshall's ear, but the boy backed away. *Talk to your mom goddamnit*, he thought.

When Marshall would not speak, Jace whispered goodbye to Lynne, and did what he always did in these desperate situations. He hugged Marshall, pulling the boy's face against his chest.

***

When Lynne got home from the hospital, she showered and they both got into bed. They lay in the dark, and he could smell her, the charcoal soap, tea-tree oil shampoo. He reached out and took her hand in his.

"The card was declined at the hospital," she said. "We're lucky that they agreed to mail the bill."

"Why didn't you use the other ones?"

"All four cards are maxed," Lynne said.

"They can't be maxed."

"Two hundred a week just for physical therapy. A hundred for speech. Another hundred for that play therapist." She placed one hand to Jace's cheek and another to his chest. "If it was a good place. A really good place. A respected institution. We could both go back to work. Pay off our debts. Maybe even save a little."

Jace looked into her eyes, projecting a gentleness that conveyed affection, but made clear his unwillingness to negotiate. "We'll find a school," he said.

"Something new isn't just going to pop up."

"We'll move."

"Move?" she said, her face splotching. "The creditors are calling the banks about the house."

"We'll figure something out."

"Stop saying that," she said. "Why do you say that? You don't believe it. I don't believe it. There's nothing to figure out. This is what it is."

"What do you want from me?"

"Start by admitting that we're out of options."

"They have to take him back," Jace said. "One of those schools has to take him back. I'm sure of it. He can't *not* go to school."

"They told us to our faces," she said. "'We don't

want a student like Marshall.' They literally said that. I know you say it's 'discrimination,' but so what? Lawyers cost money. We don't have money. Even if you find some lawyer who is cheap and they *could* get Marshall back in school, I don't want him to go back to those places. He won't learn anything. They'll sit him in a corner all day with Duplos. Or they'll lock him in a closet. They'll call him an animal. They'll blame us for his behavior. One of their aides is going to hurt him, I guarantee you. Or they're going to call the police and they'll stun him or worse, shoot him."

"That's a little much."

"Do you even read those articles I forward you?" Her face was reddening into something that wasn't frustration with the argument, but exasperation with something much larger. "Cops shoot kids like Marshall all the time! The point is that we haven't been able to afford his physical therapist for months. You can't keep tying him up to that tree or locking him in the shed. Someone is going to call social services one day. They'll take Marshall away. Mark my words."

"And you think one of these institutions will be better?" he said, his voice rising. "You've seen what I've seen. You see what happens to kids in places like that. Listen, I'll call the school on Monday. They might have changed their mind. We can ask them to make adjustments. They just need more resources. Proper resources."

Jace climbed out of bed and stood, shifting on his feet as if the floorboards were hot from the sun.

"Please," she said. "I'm begging you."

"I will not put our son in an institution," he said. "I can handle a bad school. Yes. I can handle that." Jace gathered his next words carefully. "We have to just keep going forward."

"You're in denial."

He ran his hand over his face, scraping stubble. "We're still standing, for all I can see. We're healthy. We have all our arms and legs. You talk as if we've lost this fight."

Lynne's eyes narrowed, nostrils flaring. There was a defensiveness to her gaze. Jace hated it when Lynne looked at him like that. It was unfair, almost condescending.

"This is it," she said. "This is our one life. Putting up this goddamn endless fight. Think about it, Jace. If this is all we have, then do you want to spend it caring for a child that exhausts us emotionally and physically? Don't look at me like that. Please. I started out good. You know I did. I gave that boy everything I had. Every hour. Every minute. Marsh grew, but he didn't grow like other kids. So, I said I just want him to be independent. To be able to care for himself once you and I were gone. When I saw that wasn't going to happen either, I tried to stop his tantrums. At least, if I could stop his tantrums and he was institutionalized, he wouldn't get hurt by the staff. And when that didn't work, when I couldn't stop the Fury and the Panic, I don't know."

"You gave up."

"What else is there to do?"

"You make him sound stuck. I don't think he's stuck. There's a boy there. You know it. You…you've just lost sight of it because of all those people outside…all those other voices. You love that boy there and so do I."

Her face was wet, but Jace recognized that they were not tears of acceptance, but of exhaustion.

"He's still the same boy he was when he was three," she said. "I know you see it differently. You taught Marshall how to survive in the wilderness. Fishing. Hunting. But what good does that do us here? He can't legally live outside. And that's you and him. That's not me. I don't have what you two have."

"That's the point," Jace said. "If he can learn to survive in the wilderness, then he can learn to survive here, in town."

"I don't think it's the same."

"Of course it is. It's hard up there on the mountain.

You gave me those books. The ones about hermits and outcasts. Those guys were all on the spectrum. Even Kid Colter lived to be seventy or something. And…and he was nonverbal. It's a sign. Don't you get it? Marsh can learn. Just because *we* can't see how, doesn't mean it can't happen."

Lynne sat down on the edge of the bed and stared at herself in the dressing mirror. She was wearing satin pajamas that hung from her bony body, her hair was wet from being washed, her nails were chipped, her skin opaque. She had been raised a healthy mountain girl, ruddy-cheeked and without a care. It struck him how much the last decade had taken from her.

"I need a break," she said. "That's all I'm asking. And I want to take that break with you. Just the two of us."

"We have a child, babe. Parents can't take breaks."

"Jace," she said softly. "All I'm asking for is a couple years. We'll visit him every day. We'll rebuild. Put this house back together." After taking a minute to gather herself, she said, "If we don't take a break, we'll lose our house anyway. Don't you see that's our future if we keep going like this? You have stamina. I don't. The bills. The sleepless nights. The tantrums. I can't just go and go like you do. I really can't."

XIV

There was barking, continuous and sharp. It stopped and Jace was relieved that he could drift back to sleep. Then someone shouted.

"*Dad!*"

The plugged entrance to the snow hut had been knocked down and the blue sky burst through, honing a spotlight into their cocoon. When Jace opened his eyes, Elway was there, gazing down at him. He shifted his head and beyond Elway, through the entryway, glimpsed a young boy, a teenager whose mouth and nose were covered in a red ski mask.

"*Dad!*" the boy shouted again, the word sounding as if it came from underwater.

There was movement and Jace heard another voice, one that had beckoned him when he was a child, whispering through the darkness of a pillow fort or calling out from the back of an abandoned mine. The boy yanked off his ski mask, revealing a younger version of Ozzie's face. He checked Jace's pulse, then checked Marshall's, stroked their necks, inspected fingers and noses, rambling the whole time.

Ozzie appeared behind the teenager, moving him gently to the side, and fell upon Jace, hugging him and pouring hot breath against his friend's ear, choking through every other word. His grip was too hard, his weight pressing against Jace's sternum.

Ozzie reached into his backpack, dug out a medical body heater, and put it into Jace and Marshall's sleeping bag. Jace immediately felt warmth against his skin as Ozzie switched on the power.

Ozzie's son, Jeremy, was beyond the entrance, speaking into a radio while waving his hands into the sky. Time went and came in terrific thrusts, as if rioting against steady movement. There was a terrific roar echoing between the turret-like peaks, a noise so loud that it threatened the fragile stability of their snow cave. A shadow passed over, a spinning meteor that was gone as quickly as it had arrived.

Jace could barely open his eyes. *Frostbite*, he thought. He tried to move, but his body would not respond. He turned to Marshall. His son's chest shuddered and his lungs gulped for air.

Ozzie called to Jeremy, opened a medic bag, inserted an IV into Marshall's arm, and handed the transparent bag back to his son. He placed an oxygen mask over Marshall's mouth, hands trembling. Ozzie's cheeks were reddening, his nose pale and waxen, his tears disappearing into his beard.

They heard a distant rumbling, the sound of blades cutting through the air. A shining red and white machine appeared against the blue sky, lowering itself slowly like a giant bee above a flower. Snow was blowing everywhere as the massive machine steadied feet above the ground. A small man and a large woman jumped out of the helicopter's bay. They were uneasy on the slope and staggered forward carrying stretchers. Marshall was motionless through it all, eyes shut, Suzy clutched in his hand.

"Faith," Ozzie whispered in Jace's ear. Jace forced a smile, but he couldn't feel his cheeks or lips.

They carefully dragged Jace and Marshall from the snow hut, loaded them onto stretchers, lifted then locked them in the bay of the helicopter. The helicopter shuddered and swung and slowly they rose out over the mountain. Jace noticed staggered lines of volunteers far below, wearing matching neon-orange reflectors, men and women who had come out to find Leslie, Jace, and Marshall.

The helicopter made a sharp turn and soon they were flying along the side of the mountain. Every crevice and crook of the snow-covered peaks was illuminated by the rising sun. Jace closed his eyes against the light. He still felt the enormous presence of the mountain, vast, immutable, permanent.

He had to stay focused. He could not lose consciousness. Not now. So he turned his head and looked at Marshall and directed a simple thought, one that he knew the boy could hear, even without the words.

"*I'm still here…*"

ACKNOWLEDGMENTS

I'd like to thank my editor, Anne Terashima, for her patience, kindness, and thoroughness, and Kirsten Johanna Allen for taking on this story and reviving my trust in publishing. Philip Turner for his gentle guidance through many drafts, Leslie Gardner for years of advice and support, Wouter Bongers for help with the medical details, and Godert de Wit for reading. I'd especially like to thank Jikke for, well, everything—a man like me couldn't ask for a more supportive and loving wife. I'd also like to thank one of the best sons a father could ask for, Casjen, a younger brother forced to be a big one, and Falk, who is too young to see autism and, instead, has shown me that he can admire his older brother simply for being the hero he is. I'd also like to thank my father, Carl, for his unending encouragement with my writing, and Sunny, Caspar and Els, for all the care and kindness given not only to me, but to my boys as well.

ABOUT THE AUTHOR

Erik Raschke received an MA in Creative Writing from the City College of New York. His first novel, *The Book of Samuel*, was translated into Italian and nominated for the Michael L. Printz Award. His work has appeared in *The Atlantic*, *The New York Times Magazine*, *Guernica*, and elsewhere. Originally from Denver, Colorado, Raschke became a dual Dutch and American citizen in 2013. He teaches writing at the University of Amsterdam.

ABOUT THE COVER

Cover art by David Shingler

Mount Herard of the Sangre De Cristo. San Luis Valley, Colorado. 36"x48" Oil on wood.

Inspired broadly by the dramatic landscapes of the West, all the way to the open fields and ocean vistas of the East Coast, David Shingler integrates these influences into his personal technique and painting style. He says of his inspiration, "I am captivated by vast open space and mesmerized by majestic snowy peaks." He specializes in painting oil on wood panels, which he personally builds. Shingler's oil paintings are not photorealistic, but they create a sense of depth and energy that often makes viewers feel they are in the landscape. Having resided for five years in Denver, Shingler devoted time to exploring Colorado and the neighboring states; western landscapes are his favorite painting subjects. The overwhelming natural beauty of the West continues to inspire him.

Visit www.davidshingler.com to view more of Shingler's work.

TORREY HOUSE PRESS

Voices for the Land

The economy is a wholly owned subsidiary of the environment, not the other way around.
—Senator Gaylord Nelson, founder of Earth Day

Torrey House Press publishes books at the intersection of the literary arts and environmental advocacy. THP authors explore the diversity of human experiences and relationships with place. THP books create conversations about issues that concern the American West, landscape, literature, and the future of our ever-changing planet, inspiring action toward a more just world. We believe that lively, contemporary literature is at the cutting edge of social change. We seek to inform, expand, and reshape the dialogue on environmental justice and stewardship for the natural world by elevating literary excellence from diverse voices.

Visit www.torreyhouse.org for reading group discussion guides, author interviews, and more.

As a 501(c)(3) nonprofit publisher, our work is made possible by the generous donations of readers like you.

Torrey House Press is supported by Back of Beyond Books, the King's English Bookshop, Jeff Adams and Heather Adams, the Jeffrey S. and Helen H. Cardon Foundation, Diana Allison, Jerome Cooney and Laura Storjohann, Robert Aagard and Camille Bailey Aagard, Heidi Dexter and David Gens, Kirtly Parker Jones, the Utah Division of Arts & Museums, Utah Humanities, the National Endowment for the Humanities, the National Endowment for the Arts, and Salt Lake County Zoo, Arts & Parks. Our thanks to individual donors, subscribers, and the Torrey House Press board of directors for their valued support.

Join the Torrey House Press family and give today at www.torreyhouse.org/give.